"Umm-hmm," Rachel mumbled, determined not to open her mouth

She should stop him. Say no. Do something.

But she stood there as Colin started to spread the frosting over her top lip. She stared at him, transfixed. Even with all the time she'd spent in Marco's kitchen, Marco had never done anything this erotic.

He'd never touched her like this, making her quiver with anticipation.

Sex had been basic. Ordinary. Bland.

Nothing like the high intensity of this moment.

This was sweeter than any dessert. This was pure bliss.

Dear Reader,

I love to cook. Cakes, pies and pastries are my all-time favorites to bake, especially if the main ingredient is chocolate. I have dozens of cookbooks in my kitchen, and I dug out my favorites when I needed inspiration for this book. While I haven't made the cupcakes that bring about sparks between Rachel Palladia and Colin Morris, I have made the coconut cake that Rachel brings to Easter brunch.

After her engagement to a New York City restaurateur ends, pastry chef Rachel returns to Morrisville, Indiana. Instead of being able to get legal advice from Bruce Lancaster (*Legally Tender*, American Romance 1100), Rachel finds that her only hope for keeping the recipes she developed out of the hands of her ex-fiancé is Colin Morris, the boy next door and her former childhood crush. She, Bruce and Colin were best friends, until Colin stood her up for the prom.

But Colin's behavior was the result of a big misunderstanding. Rachel and Colin quickly discover that when you mix two former next-door-neighbors together and simmer over a rekindled flame, you just might have the perfect recipe for marriage.

Happy reading, and enjoy the romance. And feel free to contact me through my Web site, www.micheledunaway.com.

Michele Dunaway

The Marriage Recipe
MICHELE DUNAWAY

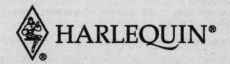

HARLEQUIN®

TORONTO • NEW YORK • LONDON
AMSTERDAM • PARIS • SYDNEY • HAMBURG
STOCKHOLM • ATHENS • TOKYO • MILAN • MADRID
PRAGUE • WARSAW • BUDAPEST • AUCKLAND

ISBN-13: 978-0-373-75211-9
ISBN-10: 0-373-75211-3

THE MARRIAGE RECIPE

Printed in U.S.A.

ABOUT THE AUTHOR

In first grade Michele Dunaway knew she wanted to be a teacher when she grew up, and by second grade she knew she wanted to be an author. By third grade she was determined to be both, and before her high school class reunion, she'd succeeded. In addition to writing romance, Michele is a nationally recognized English and journalism educator who also advises both the yearbook and newspaper at her school. Born and raised in a west county suburb of St. Louis, Missouri, Michele has traveled extensively, with the cities and places she's visited often becoming settings for her stories. Described as a woman who does too much but doesn't ever want to stop, Michele gardens five acres in her spare time and shares her house with two young daughters and five extremely lazy house cats and one rambunctious kitten that rule the roost.

Books by Michele Dunaway

HARLEQUIN AMERICAN ROMANCE

*American Beauties

For Chris Waldo.
The sky's the limit and you're conquering that!
I'm proud of all you've accomplished.

And for Marty Smith,
my brother and chef extraordinaire;
and to my fantastic editor Beverley Sotolov,
who helped make this book one of my favorites.

Chapter One

Rachel Palladia was up to her elbows in dough. Unfortunately, none of it was green—the kind she really needed. Specifically, one-hundred-dollar bills, and lots of them.

Damn it all. No, damn *him.* Rachel let the curse word fly as she thought of her thirty-six-year-old fiancé, Marco Alessandro. Make that *ex*-fiancé. A woman simply did not marry a man to whom faithfulness meant he could sample the sous chef whenever his libido demanded it.

"I'm Italian," Marco had proclaimed when she'd caught him and the nubile sous chef buck naked and bopping like rabbits in Rachel's bed. "Italian men take mistresses. You will always have my heart. You will be my wife."

Rachel had uttered a few choice expletives, tossed his diamond ring at him, told him to get out of her life and her apartment—and promptly donated her bed and linens to Goodwill. She was sleeping on one of those inflatable single mattresses until she could afford something else, but at least the inflatable was pure, unsoiled.

Rachel sighed, slapped the white-flour blob on the stainless-steel worktable and used a rolling pin to smooth out the piecrust. She was out several thousand dollars in nonrefundable deposits for wedding items and there were charges on her credit cards for other nonreturnable ones.

Even worse was that she was still working for the son of— Rachel bit off the word. Her mom insisted that ever since Rachel had moved to New York City at eighteen she'd started cussing like a sailor. Rachel planned on cleaning up her language, but this fiasco with Marco wasn't helping any.

She placed the rolled-out dough in the pie pans and began trimming the crusts. To have come this far only to come to this… Rachel resisted the urge to throw the excess dough. She'd been in food service all her life, beginning at her grandmother's diner in Morrisville, Indiana. Instead of attending college, Rachel had graduated from the CIA— Culinary Institute of America, that is—then worked her way up in a succession of kitchen jobs until she'd landed here as head pastry chef at Alessandro's, a fine Italian restaurant on Manhattan's Upper West Side.

God knows how many other women had revolved in and out of Marco's life before she'd caught him with the sous chef one week before Valentine's Day.

She'd spent the holiday of love alone, nursing her wounds and chastising herself for missing the signs. She had to be an idiot. That mistress stuff only happened on TV, or so she'd thought. Now she was stuck in an employment contract with a noncompete clause that wouldn't allow her to work within fifty miles of the restaurant. Which left out finding another job in New York City, a town she'd loved from the very first minute she'd stepped foot in Penn Station the summer she'd been eighteen. Unless Marco let her out of her contract she had no option but to keep on at Alessandro's if she wanted to stay in any of the five boroughs.

New York had vibes rural Morrisville didn't. Sure, the

tall buildings hid the sun. But the neon lights and nonstop crowds generated an energy that inspired. Despite being mostly anonymous in this city of over eight million people, she'd never felt rejected, as she had during her high-school days at home.

"So, are you surviving?" Glynnis, Rachel's second in command, took the pie pans from Rachel and began adding the rich chocolate filling.

"I'm fine," Rachel replied. She tucked the bangs of her dark brown hair under her pink baseball cap. She preferred something less ornate than those big white chef hats. "It's definitely been the week from hell. Thankfully, Marco took that last-minute trip to Italy. I'm finally ready to face him when he returns today."

"You think he's man enough to own up to what he did and still work with you?" Glynnis asked. The pies now filled, the older woman put them into the oven.

Many restaurants bought their desserts from specialty companies, but Alessandro's baked everything on the premises. In fact, over the past two years, Rachel's desserts had become so popular that the restaurant had now sold them to patrons and other dining establishments. When she'd dated Marco, she'd enjoyed helping him grow the family business this way. He'd told her that once they were married she'd receive half his stake in the restaurant. He'd insisted that married couples shared everything. He was lucky he hadn't passed along some sort of STD to Rachel in his spirit of sharing.

Rachel suppressed her anger. She couldn't believe she'd been so naive in the twenty-first century. But she'd wanted that alpha-male fairy tale. How stupid to have fallen for a lie—that his type of man was perfect for her.

She'd deal with the bas— him, she amended, when he came in to work today. She prayed she was ready.

YOU COULD TELL when Marco Alessandro was in the building. Six foot two, charismatic, he had movie-star looks that made women swoon. He arrived promptly at four, greeted his staff and then made certain everything was ready for the dinner rush, which began when the restaurant opened at five. By six, there would be an hour's wait for a table, because unless you knew one of the Alessandro family personally or were a favored regular, Alessandro's didn't take reservations. Even celebrities had to wait at the bar.

"Ah, Rachel." Marco approached as Rachel was pulling the last of tomorrow's cakes out of the oven. Her shift would end at seven. Several heads swiveled in their direction. The sous chef was long gone, having tendered her resignation the day after Rachel had interrupted the affair. Marco leaned forward and kissed Rachel lightly on the cheek. She kept her gaze focused on the far wall, noticing that, like always, he smelled of spicy aftershave and minty breath. "You are a sight for sore eyes. I've missed you. Let's go talk in my office."

Rachel set the cake pans down on the cooling rack and followed him as requested, noting he was impeccably dressed in a custom black Armani suit—his standard work attire.

His presence would dominate both the dining area and the kitchen. He would supervise everything, greet patrons at each table, and raise toasts to special events. He'd made Alessandro's one of New York's dining destinations. His brother Anthony preferred to stay behind the scenes and kept office hours, managing the operational things like payroll. Marco shut the door behind him and gestured for Rachel to sit. Unlike many restaurant offices, this one could easily suit any law firm or Fortune 100 company. The space was not as huge as his brother Anthony's office, but the mahogany furniture gave off that air of old-money wealth and privilege, although Marco came from neither. He took his rightful place behind his desk, leaned back in his leather chair and stared at her. "Have you calmed down yet?" he asked bluntly.

She cocked her head and her brow wrinkled. "Calmed down?" she repeated, incredulous, her blood pressure rising at his insinuation that their rift was her fault.

"Yes. I assumed my week away would allow you some time to put that unfortunate incident behind you. I, too, have done some thinking, and perhaps my words were not as clear as I'd meant them to be."

She bristled. "Not clear? What's not clear? You were having sex with the sous chef in our bed—my bed—and then telling me that all Italian men have affairs."

Marco adjusted his red power tie. "Yes, well, maybe that was a little inconsiderate of me."

"You think?" Rachel retorted.

He didn't seem too perturbed. "I forget that you have Italian blood. It's what makes you so fiery. I dallied. I was wrong. From here forward, I will be committed. I don't want this relationship to end."

"Perhaps you should have thought about that before you bopped a bimbo," Rachel snapped, her anger boiling. "Marriage is sacred. My parents were married for thirty-two years before my father's heart attack. My grandparents' marriage lasted over fifty. Until death do us part. Monogamy. Faithfulness. Those things are important to me. I trusted you."

"And you can again," Marco said, as if doing so was just that easy. "We're well suited. My mother likes you. My brother raves about your pastries and how you've helped our restaurant become so in demand. My sister has never tolerated a woman in my life and yet she befriended you. We fit, Rachel. I don't want to lose you. Please forgive me."

She noticed he hadn't mentioned anything about love. She was twenty-nine, but that didn't mean she was afraid of the big three-oh when her birthday arrived in mid-April. Somehow she'd fallen for the smart image that he'd created in his attempt to rise above his middle-class Brooklyn upbringing. That was probably the true extent of his appeal. The revelation smarted. "I think the bloom is already off the rose," she told him.

"I don't understand," Marco said. He reached into his jacket pocket and drew out a small black box. "Here's your ring. I had it cleaned. I want you back by my side, where you belong."

Rachel twisted her hands into her chef's apron. When she'd first met Marco, he'd charmed the socks off her. He'd brought flowers, wined and dined her, giving her little pieces of Tiffany jewelry just because. He'd never skimped on his extravagance.

He was older than her by seven years; he'd just turned thirty-six. She'd found him worldly and wise. On his arm she'd felt like a princess and that New York City was her kingdom. He'd taken her to glamorous parties and theater premieres, shown her a world that was such a far cry from Morrisville, Indiana, where the most exciting thing was either cosmic bowling, bingo night at the Knights of Columbus hall or a dance at the country club.

She'd found Morrisville claustrophobic, but her parents

and grandparents had loved the town. Her mother and grandmother still did and were exceedingly content. At this point in her life, Rachel was not. She'd thought that perhaps marrying Marco would change that. How wrong she'd been. Instead, he'd made her unhappiness worse.

She took off her cap and undid her ponytail, letting the dark, straight locks fall around her shoulders. She was one-quarter Italian, although she considered herself first and foremost simply an American. Heritage wasn't really that important, except perhaps to the man sitting across from her.

"Marco, do you love me?" she asked.

He blinked. "What kind of question is that?" His tone bordered on indignant. "Of course I do. I asked you to marry me. Do you think I didn't have an array of women to pick from? I wouldn't have chosen you had you not been special. I love you."

Rachel sat there, arms folded across her chest. Marco was smart enough not to approach her. Normally after a fight, he'd hug her, run his fingers through her hair and whisper words that made everything better. If he tried any of those now, she'd slug him. No, how Marco really felt was clear. She'd be a big fool if she thought Marco was marrying her for anything but to protect his bottom line and his profits.

"I can't marry you," she told him.

Surprised, he frowned. "What? Your ring is right here. Just slide it back on and we'll call the priest and let him know we still need our date. Anything you've canceled can easily be restarted. I'll spare no expense."

The offer was pointless. As much as zebras couldn't change their stripes, Marco couldn't change, either. She sighed.

"Marco, be honest. You don't really love me. You like that I'm convenient. I'm a great chef. Your family accepts me. But I can't ever trust you again. I can't even fathom touching you with a ten-foot pole. It's better to put this behind us and move on."

A vein twitched in his forehead. "You'll make a fool of me," he said, revealing the real reason he was still insistent on the marriage.

She shook her head, disagreeing. "People end engagements all the time. There might be a little press, but that's not necessarily a bad thing. You're Marco Alessandro. You'll spin this news into more sales of calamari and caviar."

He tapped his fingertips, his elbows firmly planted on the desk. His mouth edged downward. "I was afraid you were going to be stubborn. Anthony worried that you might be. He suggested I see my lawyer before I left for Italy."

"Lawyer?" Rachel said, her eyebrows arching in shock. Anthony had made a point to avoid her since the "event." So what was Marco trying to do—get her on a breach of contract? She'd given him back the ring. She didn't owe him one darn dime. If anything, he owed her.

"You have a contract with Alessandro's," Marco said, his voice level. "As long as you were my fiancée, that contract was merely a piece of paper. A formality. Now that you no longer plan on marrying me, Anthony insists that I…the restaurant, I mean…well, I suppose all of us must protect ourselves."

"Anthony," she said. "What is it that he wants? Are you firing me?"

"No, no," Marco said quickly. He grabbed the ring box and tucked the diamond back into his pocket. "I have no desire for you to leave. Neither does my brother. Despite your stubbornness, I'm sure that in time you'll come to your senses and forgive me. Then all will be well and we can stop this foolishness. Until then, Anthony just wants things on the up-and-up."

"Meaning," Rachel prodded. She knew that Marco was using his brother as a ploy to make Marco appear less the bad guy.

He brushed some lint off his jacket and then locked his gaze on hers as he delivered his ultimatum. "We want you to turn over your recipes. Anything you developed here while working for Alessandro's belongs to us."

"Are you crazy?" Rachel said, jumping to her feet so that she had some height on him. She couldn't believe he'd demand such a thing. "Those are mine."

"No," Marco said with a patronizing shake of his head. "They're my recipes. Alessandro's. You created them as works for hire while we were paying you a salary. Since you don't want to marry me—well, it's all right here." From an inside pocket of his jacket he drew out a large cream-colored envelope. He placed it on his desk and slid it toward her.

Rachel could see the law firm's return address printed in the corner. Fingers trembling, she picked up the packet and removed the contents. There, in black ink, was a legal demand that she relinquish all recipes created or suffer being taken to civil court. She couldn't believe Marco had been so…premeditated. "You're giving me a demand letter?"

"It was Anthony's idea," Marco said, as if blaming his brother made the letter less of an evil. "This would all be so much simpler if you married me as we'd planned. We had a good thing going."

"Until you couldn't keep your pants zipped," Rachel

pointed out as she skimmed the appalling letter again. "I don't understand the rationale behind this action. I work for you. I bake here. My desserts feed your customers. That won't change just because you and I are no longer engaged."

"But in the future, it might. What if you choose to leave?" He tapped his fingertips again.

"I have a six-month noncompete clause," she reminded him.

"Yes, and six months is a mere drop in the ocean of time. If you go, all the money Alessandro's has invested in you flies out the window. We run a business here, and as much as I'd like to be generous, Anthony's right. We can't let you take our property with you."

Now he was talking way over her head. She planted her hands on her hips. "Let me see. Either I marry you, or I turn over my recipes?"

"Marriage to me wouldn't be that bad," Marco said with a smile. "At least you'd get something permanent in return."

"Who says I'd turn over my recipes then?" she demanded. The gall of the man.

He seemed taken aback by her outburst. "As I've always said, husbands and wives share everything. And when you became pregnant and stayed home to raise our children, your replacement would continue your work. I don't see what the big deal is."

Pregnant? Stay home and be barefoot in the kitchen? What had she seen in him? "You are archaic."

"Tradition is part of my heritage."

"Oh, please," Rachel scoffed. She was sick of the charade. "Enough of this. You're a third-generation Brooklynite whose trips to Italy are all for show. Give me a break.

You're not getting my recipes, which by the way originated from my grandmother's cookbook. Not your kitchen."

"Don't make this more difficult than it has to be," Marco said. He stood and gestured. "You're overwrought. Perhaps I shouldn't have gone to Italy. I should have wooed you more. Made amends. I'll call Anthony and have him cover for me tonight. We'll go out. See a show. You can pick out a new piece of jewelry."

"No." Rachel placed both hands on his desk and leaned forward. "This is over. You and I are through. *T-H-R-O-U-G-H*."

He stepped around the desk, as if sensing the situation was spiraling out of his control. "Rachel, please calm down. Be sensible. I'm not your enemy."

"No, Anthony is." Rachel waved the letter in front of Marco. "Well, we're not playing this game. You will not steal my recipes." She got up and stalked to the door.

"Rachel, this will get ugly," he warned.

She whirled around. "It already has," she told him. "You're an egotistical creep. The worst kind of human. I don't want to be around you. I quit."

His indignation was immediate. "You can't quit. Who will bake your cakes? And you won't work anywhere. I'll see to it."

She couldn't contain herself. "Hell hath no fury like a woman scorned. Don't kick a sleeping snake."

"You and your stupid quotations. I always hated those. You're like a walking Bartlett's."

"Good, then hate this. You can't threaten me. You have no hold over me. None. You won't get my recipes, so just leave me alone, Marco. I'm out of your life."

She stormed out of his office, and didn't realize he'd

followed her to the kitchen until she heard his footsteps behind her.

"You will not walk out of here until you give me your recipes," he shouted. "That letter says you must."

Faces appeared around stainless-steel pots and pans. The kitchen, normally a crescendo of clattering, quieted as spectators watched the show.

"You can't demand anything from me. I just quit," Rachel said, her voice notching upward.

"I can and I will," Marco warned. "You'll deal with my lawyers. Anthony's lawyers."

She rolled her eyes. "Please. Neither you nor your brother scares me. This isn't some silly TV show. It's real life. In fact—" her gaze lighted on the chocolate cakes she'd left out to cool "—you want my recipes?"

"They *are* Alessandro's property," he reiterated.

Rachel smiled. "Fine. Have them." She dug her hand into the nearest nine-inch cake pan and drew out a still-warm chunk of moist chocolate cake. Within seconds, the huge mass had found a new home on the front of Marco's suit. She stood there, defiant. Marco took one step forward, then stopped, aware of the avid audience. "Replacing my suit will come out of your final check," he said.

"In that case…" Rachel shrugged, reached into another cake pan and hurled another gob at him, this time nailing him on the neck. Brown crumbs clung to his jaw, catching on the evening stubble. "Now, that's worth every penny."

Marco glared at her but didn't say another word. Instead he turned, retreated, and moments later the door to his office slammed, the sound resonating throughout the kitchen.

The staff looked at Rachel in obvious appreciation before quickly returning to work. Only Glynnis followed

Rachel to her locker. "Never would have believed that if I hadn't seen it. You'll be the talk of the crew for days. Can't say he didn't have it coming to him."

"You've been great to work with," Rachel said, her adrenaline beginning to ebb as the reality of what she'd done crept in. She removed her Alessandro's apron and tossed it on a table.

"Call me if you ever need me," Glynnis said. "I'd come work for you anyday."

"Thanks, but I'll have to let you know. I'm somewhat unemployable at the moment." Rachel tugged her coat from her locker and grabbed her purse. She dumped the padlock and key into her bag, then she reached up to the top shelf and took down the only other item in the locker. She kept most of her recipes at her apartment, but she'd made copies of the desserts she baked for Alessandro's and stored them here in a small notebook.

"You're giving him those?" Glynnis asked.

"Hell, no," Rachel said with a wry laugh. "He's not going to sue me, and he can rot somewhere hot if he does."

"So what will you do? You don't have the money to fight him if you can't work," Glynnis said, obviously concerned.

"Oh, I've got a job waiting for me," Rachel declared, not wanting Glynnis to worry. Rachel would have to put her tail between her legs to ask for the position, but once she walked in the door, she knew the owners wouldn't turn her away.

"You got a job? Where?" Glynnis asked.

"Kim's Diner," Rachel said, the idea taking hold.

Glynnis appeared confused. "Kim's? Is it in Jersey?"

"No. Morrisville." Rachel saw her expression. "Indiana."

"Never heard of it," Glynnis admitted.

That was the kicker. "No one has." The adrenaline of the moment had worn off completely and Rachel trembled as she digested the implications of her rash decision. She'd hate leaving New York. She loved the city. She vowed to make her exile only temporary. She plastered a brave smile on her face.

"You know what the tough do when the going gets rough?" she asked.

Glynnis shook her head.

Rachel picked up her bag and gave Glynnis a hug. Hopefully, she'd see her friend soon. "The tough go home."

Chapter Two

"Who would have thought coming home would cause this much stir," Rachel said as she put away the last of the clean dishes.

"Now, don't let all the gossips get you down." Her grandmother Kim said as she handed Rachel one last plate. The diner was only open for breakfast and lunch, and as soon as longtime patron Harold Robison finished his last cup of coffee, the workday would be over. Harold liked to linger, and for years had ignored the sign indicating that Kim's closed at precisely three o'clock. "Everyone's just glad to see you, that's all."

"Yeah, that's it," Rachel told her grandmother. She'd been back in Morrisville for two full days now. Once she'd stormed out of Alessandro's, she'd been a woman of action. One day and two phone calls later and she'd had her place sublet. One more phone call had gotten her car out of its Queens storage lot. A week after tossing cake on her former fiancé, Rachel had been on the road, driving from New York to Indiana with her personal possessions loaded in the trunk.

Unfortunately, she hadn't escaped town quickly enough to avoid a courier-delivered envelope from Anthony and

Marco Alessandro's lawyer. Not only had they docked her final paycheck for the cost of replacing Marco's suit, leaving her with a mere six dollars and ten cents, but they'd also given her thirty days to turn over her recipes or face civil action.

The amount they'd valued her recipes at had been astronomical. The morning after the cake flinging, Rachel had prayed that Marco would see how stupid and silly they were both being, but apparently, he was determined to punish her.

She no longer had rent expense, but she did have credit card debt. Now she was about to add legal bills to an already stretched budget. She refused to take charity from her mother and grandmother—it was bad enough she was back in her childhood bedroom, which had pretty much remained unchanged since the day she'd left for New York City. Her window still faced the Morris house; the only difference was that Colin Morris, her friend since childhood, no longer occupied the room across the way. As youngsters, they'd used flashlights and Morse code—get it? Morse/Morris code, they'd laugh—and sent messages to each other until late at night.

For income, Rachel had negotiated eleven dollars an hour to work at Kim's. Her grandmother had wanted to pay her more, but Rachel knew that any money for a higher salary would come from her grandmother's pocket and not the restaurant's cash register. Kim Palladia lived comfortably, but Rachel didn't want to be in debt to her family. It was time she faced the music.

Starting with heading to the law office of Lancaster and Morris, which had provided legal expertise to the town of Morrisville for over fifty years.

Rachel tugged on her coat. She'd walk across Main Street, through the parking lot, and be in the law-office lobby before her bravado deserted her. She dreaded hearing what Bruce Lancaster would have to say. He was one of the sharpest legal minds in the state and a former childhood playmate, but she had to admit she was petrified he'd tell her that Marco had a legitimate claim to her recipes and she'd have to turn them over.

"I'm leaving," she called.

Her grandmother waved. "See you at home tonight," she said. She'd moved in eight years ago, adding another body to the Palladia homestead. The century-old Victorian home, which stood on a half-acre lot, was really too big for just two people. But it had been in Rachel's father's family for two generations, and Rachel's mother simply couldn't bear to part with it. Rachel knew that her mother hoped she'd eventually move home and raise a family in the old place. She hated disappointing her, but figured all those years in New York City were a clue that she didn't want to be a small-town girl.

The blustery March wind whipped down the street, causing the Easter decorations hanging from light poles to sway. Morrisville had signs for every holiday. The current ones displayed a white bunny carrying an egg-filled basket and advertised the annual Knights of Columbus Easter-egg event the middle of the month.

Rachel gathered her coat closer, and soon was inside the first set of huge wooden doors. She crossed the black-and-white tile floor and pulled on the next set. Lancaster and Morris was situated in the former county seat, an old court-houselike, three-story building complete with a rotunda. Colin Morris used to say there were two coveted offices in the place: the Morris office, which overlooked Main Street, and the Lancaster office, which overlooked the town park. Rachel strode over to the receptionist, seated behind a huge desk.

"May I help you?" the girl asked.

"I'm here to see Bruce Lancaster. If he's available," Rachel added hastily.

"Do you have an appointment?" She had to be about twenty, Rachel decided, and already she had a wedding ring on her finger.

"No." Gosh, she really was an idiot. "I'm Rachel Palladia. My grandmother owns Kim's Diner. She's a client here." Rachel had no idea whose, but Lancaster and Morris had handled both her father's and her grandfather's estates.

"Mr. Lancaster is out of town for the next two weeks," the receptionist said politely. "He and his wife—"

"Oh, yes, Christina. I didn't attend their wedding, but my mother and grandmother went." Rachel smiled helpfully. "Is she available?"

"No, she's out of town, as well. I can see who else could meet with you, if you'd like. If no one is available today, I'd be more than happy to set up an appointment for some other time."

Rachel sighed with frustration. She'd have better luck just walking next door this evening, bringing Reginald Morris an apple pie and asking for his advice after dinner. "No, that's okay. I'll take care of it."

She turned and began the trek back across the marble floor, the rubber soles of her tennis shoes squeaking. She'd just reached the outer set of doors when one of them opened as if of its own volition. The motion threw her off balance, and she plowed right into the man walking in.

"Careful there," he said, his bare hand catching her arm in an attempt to steady her. His wool overcoat slapped around his legs and his briefcase banged his knee. "Gotta look where you're going," he chastised her lightly.

"I was," Rachel replied, her patience a tad on the thin side.

"As long as you're okay," he said. It was then that they both took a good look at each other. "Rachel?" the man said. "It *is* you."

Colin Morris stood in front of her, blocking her escape. "Hi, Colin," she replied.

He smiled. They were still in the vestibule, and he let the outer door close behind him with a thud. "It's good to see you. I heard you were in town." His blue eyes narrowed. "What are you doing here?"

"What, in town?" He hadn't grown dense over the years, had he?

He frowned. "No. Here. Where I work."

"Oh. I wanted to catch Bruce, but he's away."

"Yeah, his wife's pregnant and soon she won't be able to travel with Bella, her little girl. Christina and Bruce decided to visit her side of the family now, while she's still mobile.

"So, you're home for a while?" he asked conversationally.

"Yes. You know, I do come home occasionally. In fact, I was home this past Christmas," she said, chafing. "I met Christina then. She came briefly into Kim's to pick up some of my mom's chicken salad. I'm in and out so quickly that I don't have time to see everyone. Most of my friends are all married and busy with their own lives. I have managed to keep in touch with Heather."

"Yeah, but not with me or Bruce. You didn't attend his wedding. I thought I'd run into you there. We haven't caught up in years."

"I was in the Hamptons that weekend with a prior commitment."

"Oh." He arched his eyebrows disapprovingly, as if he found hobnobbing a poor excuse for missing a friend's nuptials.

Rachel exhaled, blowing a strand of wind-tossed hair off her face. She didn't want to get into any discussion with Colin here, in between doorways. The man had no right to judge her. She might be back in Morrisville, but the friendship they'd shared was long past. She was all grown-up now, and not so enamored with Colin's playboy ways.

"It's been great catching up, Colin, but I've really got to get back. Kim's closes at three, but there's always cleaning to do. I said I'd help."

"You're working there now?" he asked.

She gritted her teeth. "Temporarily. I have a few matters to take care of, which is why I came by to consult Bruce. I'll just visit your dad tonight. Take him and your mom a pie."

"He always had a sweet spot for you and your desserts," Colin said with a laugh. When he grinned, the harsh angles of his face softened. He could frown and remain drop-dead attractive; smiling made him a heartthrob. Sadly, even after all the years away, Rachel found herself not immune. He had been her secret crush for so long. That had to be the reason she experienced a tingle in her toes and a shiver along her spine. The man was simply magnetic. Like Marco, Colin probably affected a lot of other women this way.

"So what do you want to talk to Dad about?" he asked, pushing the inner door open. "I've got some time and we're blocking the exit. We need to either go one way or the other. Why don't you tell me about it."

"Really, I'm not going to be here in Morrisville that long and—"

He stopped, his foot holding open the lobby door. "Look, Rachel, if it's something legal, my father has a pretty tight schedule for the next few weeks. He's due in court two days from now as the defense counsel in what's shaping up to be a huge and long trial. If you want some advice, I'll help. We are still friends, aren't we?"

She wavered. Friends. That was all they'd been until her heart had gotten in the way. Even afterward, the feelings had been one-sided. Hers.

Oh, she'd once made the mistake of thinking that he'd asked her out, but it had been only one of those "in passing" things that people say to be polite. She and Colin had snuck outside with a half-size bottle of pink champagne. The liquor had made her fuzzy, and they'd kissed, but that had been it. Nothing more.

The next day, life had returned to normal and she hadn't needed a prom dress after all—at least, not until her senior year. By then, Colin and Bruce were college sophomores at Indiana University. The girl next door could never compete with the sophisticated girls the two dated. After her high-school graduation, Rachel had turned her back on Morrisville and headed east.

"Are you coming?" Colin asked.

Rachel stared at him. Same blond hair, blue eyes. Same sexy-as-all-get-out grin. But she was older. Wiser. Colin no longer meant anything to her. All she wanted was her recipes and Marco Alessandro put in his place. Bruce wasn't available, and Colin could help her. She'd at least listen to what the man had to say. That didn't cost a thing.

As COLIN PUSHED the elevator button for the third floor, he remained extremely aware of Rachel. Even though they hadn't spoken walking across the lobby, he'd sensed exactly where she was behind him. He'd heard during a partner meeting yesterday that she'd returned—gossip in Morrisville traveled faster than lightning. Tongues had wagged about how Rachel had been engaged to some hotshot restaurateur in New York and she'd said good riddance to him.

"I'm down here," he said as the elevator doors opened. His corner suite was on the Morris side of the building and had a bird's-eye view of Main Street, including Kim's Diner. Two years ago faulty wiring had caused the diner to burn to the ground, leaving little but a large pile of ashes. He'd expected Rachel to come home then, but she hadn't. Thus he suspected there was more behind her current relocation. Colin hung up his jacket.

"Can I get that?" he asked.

"No, I'm fine," Rachel said, removing her coat and sitting in the wingback chair across from his desk.

So she was still stubborn. That hadn't changed.

"I like your office," she said.

"Thanks," he said politely, drinking in the changes to her appearance. Growing up, she'd always worn her hair in a bob. Now it had grown out to past her shoulders, and she'd swept her bangs off her face. The longer style suited her. She'd filled out nicely, as well, he noticed. The red, long-sleeved Henley fit like a glove.

"Do Bruce and Christina have offices up here, too?" Rachel asked, bringing her attention from the surroundings to him.

Always Bruce, Colin thought. Rachel's hair was different, but her fascination with his friend hadn't changed. Bruce would visit the Morris household and within five minutes Rachel would be knocking on the back door. Not that he or Bruce had minded. For years, she'd simply been one of the boys, but eventually they'd reached their teens and nature had interfered. Rachel had developed the biggest crush on Bruce.

Rather inconvenient, playing second fiddle. Only in college had Colin stepped out of Bruce's shadow, at least with the ladies. As a lawyer, he'd never have the great legal mind his friend possessed, but Colin had made his peace with that and had carved out a decent career. Bruce actually had been passed over for a senior partnership when the firm had hired Christina, and now that Bruce had been promoted, Colin knew he was finally next in line.

"Their offices are in the south wing. The Lancaster end. So," he said with a deliberate cough to clear his tight throat, "what's going on?"

Rachel twisted around, the material of her sweater stretching tight. Colin swallowed and shifted. Darn, but this grown-up version of his childhood buddy had his libido roaring to life, and somehow his immediate reaction was profound and, darn it, uncomfortable. She wasn't even sending him signals, and here he was, grateful that he was safely sitting behind his desk.

She removed a wadded-up envelope from her purse, leaned over the edge of his desk and pushed the paper toward him as if touching it had burned her fingertips. Bright red polish, Colin saw. She'd worn pale pink in the past, and he wondered if her toenails were the same shade of red.

"You probably heard I was engaged," Rachel said, and he lifted his gaze to her brown eyes. That was a mistake.

Anger mixed with hurt radiated there, and Colin had the immediate urge to kill the guy who had wronged her. He retrieved the envelope and removed its contents.

"Go on," he prodded when she stopped speaking. "I'm listening and skimming this at the same time."

"Airing this is awkward. Marco Alessandro, my ex-fiancé *and* former employer, is demanding my recipes. He says he's going to sue me for them. He's claiming they're rightfully his. The bastard didn't even give me the letter until after I refused to marry him. As if."

Colin waited. Rachel had always been like a shadow. Present yet unnoticed. Her New York experience had her cursing, and as visible as the neon in Times Square. The change was mesmerizing and worth study.

"Sorry," Rachel said with a dismissive wave. "My language has taken a turn for the gutter since leaving Morrisville. Both my mother and grandmother want to wash my mouth out, but I'm too big now for them to hold down. They'd try if they could, because my mother says I swear like a sailor. I'm working on it. I've just been so agitated lately."

"It's okay," Colin said, smoothing out the demand letter and setting the legal missive aside. "I can understand. You said Marco was your fiancé."

"Yes."

"And you broke off the engagement," he went on.

"Yes."

He sat still and waited for her to elaborate. She held his gaze for a moment, blinked, then turned her head so she could study the bookcase. He didn't think she was really interested in any of the legal titles shelved there. "Rachel," he prompted. "You have to be honest with me. If I'm to help you, I've got to know everything."

"I broke off my engagement because he, he…" Her entire body shook as she relived the horror of that moment. "I caught him."

Experience had taught him patience. He waited.

She stared at him, her brown eyes imploring him not to make her do this. "Do I have to say it? Are you that much of a sadist? I caught him—in my bed—with another woman."

Had Marco Alessandro been sitting in his office, Colin would have leaped across the desk and throttled the guy with his bare hands. How dare anyone do this to Rachel? The fact that he cared this much after all these years shook him a little. And unlike those wannabe black belts, Colin legitimately was one. He'd found martial-arts training a great way to stay fit and hone both his mind and body.

Lawyers weren't supposed to be emotionally involved, but they could be empathetic. "I'm sorry," he said finally.

"Thank you," Rachel replied, the quiver of her jaw almost unnoticeable. "I have bills to pay from the canceled wedding. I returned the ring. He's not getting any more of my future. Those were my grandmother's recipes before I got them. Sure, I modified them using the restaurant's kitchen, but that doesn't mean he can take them. I need those. If I'm ever going to open my own place."

"I'll take the case," Colin said. "If he's serious about taking you to court, we may have to pull in a co-counsel licensed in New York, but your situation won't escalate that far."

He didn't know that for certain, but he had a strong suspicion. He'd never really wanted to be a lawyer and hadn't passed the bar exam with a high score, but once Colin had embraced the family profession, he had discovered that he could help people solve their problems. He'd become good at reading people and finding their weakness.

"Men like Marco Alessandro are often simply big bullies who expect the weak to roll over and give them what they want," he told her.

"What he really wants is to marry me and avoid the scandal," Rachel said, twisting her hands together in her lap.

Colin couldn't help himself. An incredulous expression registered on his face. "Is the man nuts?"

He realized his mistake the moment the words passed his lips. "Oh, Rachel. I didn't mean... I'm sorry." He'd meant the scandal part being crazy. This wasn't the Regency era. People dissolved their relationships all the time.

But his apology was too late. Her features contorted and her skin whitened. Oh, she wouldn't. He hated tears. The Rachel of old would chew off her finger before she'd ever let him see her cry.

As her tears fell, Colin suddenly realized that perhaps he'd never known the woman sitting across from him at all.

SHE WAS CRYING. Sobbing, actually. She'd gone through at least three tissues—she figured having a box around was standard procedure in a legal office—and she was about to go through her fourth as she blew her nose and sounded like a deranged goose.

Why did she have to break down here of all places? Sure she'd cried. But in private. When she'd called her good friends, she'd been tough and unyielding. She'd swallowed her pride and moved home, dealing with the endless pity and sympathy of both her family and townsfolk. Poor Rachel. How terrible a thing to have happened to her. Through it all, she'd held her head high.

Until Colin Morris. He was as insensitive as ever. And darn him, he was the only one who'd pierced the armor shielding her bruised dignity and wounded dreams.

He'd moved around his desk and squatted on the floor beside her. "I'm sorry," he repeated. "I meant the scandal. Not marrying you. Of course any man would want to marry you."

"Yeah, which is why he was sleeping around!" Rachel shouted, needing to vent. "Do you know what that's like? Finding out that everything you believed to be true is a big fat lie? That you aren't good enough? Never were? That while you thought you had passion, it obviously wasn't enough to keep a man from straying? You wouldn't understand. You're never in a relationship long enough to have your heart smashed into smithereens."

"I'll do what I can to help," Colin promised. He placed his hand reassuringly on her jean-covered thigh. "You'll get through this. You're one of the bravest and toughest people I know."

"Ha!" She sniffled. "That's why I fell apart here. I don't see you for years and first thing I do is bawl my eyes out and sob like a freak. This is why I wanted to see Bruce."

Colin straightened, placing some distance between Rachel and him. "He's not available—I am. Do you want me to handle this for you or not?"

She sniffled again, frowned at his abrupt change in tone and stared at him through what had to be red eyes. "You already know everything. You might as well take the case on. How much will it cost? I'll be honest. I'm close to broke. All my savings went to paying my credit cards. I've put the jewelry Marco gave me in a safe-deposit box just in case he starts demanding that back."

"I'll talk to my father and get back to you about the fees.

You're practically family to him, so I'm sure it won't be much. Don't stress over fees. Let me work up a response to this demand letter. Do you have copies of all the expenses you incurred preparing for your wedding?"

She nodded. "Yes."

"I'll need those," Colin said.

Rachel shifted. She'd never viewed the professional, go-get-them persona of her former next-door neighbor. She found the change fascinating. Colin was assured and confident, a man in control. He had a plan, which was more than she could say. All she'd really done was move home. Everything else she'd put on hold until she got this straightened out. "Okay, but can I ask why?"

"Absolutely. Anytime you have a question or comment you have to speak up. That's important if we're going to get the results we want. The way I see it, engagements are oral contracts. He promised to be faithful and marry you. He broke that contract. You have the right to demand that he compensate you for your mental anguish and your expenses."

"That's legal?" she asked. "There's a law regulating fidelity?"

Colin smiled. "A lot of legal maneuvering is just strategy. He demands—we demand. We negotiate a truce. If he's so worried about scandal, I doubt he wants to take this to court, where one, the suit becomes public record, and two, he risks getting an unfavorable judge, one who might have had her husband cheat on her, or a boyfriend on her daughter, or something like that."

"Ah," Rachel said, although she still didn't quite understand. Still, Colin seemed certain, and she'd always been able to trust him. "So you don't expect them to really file anything?"

He shook his head, a strand of blond hair falling across his right eye. He brushed it back, and a gold cuff link twinkled. "I don't think they will. Once court is involved, things get pricey and everyone's out a lot of money."

"Except the lawyers. I guess this is why only the lawyers get rich," Rachel said.

"Yeah, Marco's lawyer will bill for his time no matter where this goes. At this stage the case is easy money. Write a letter and send the client a bill."

"Sounds mercenary," Rachel said. "No wonder Shakespeare wrote, 'First thing we do is kill all the lawyers.'"

He shot her a look that said, *Give me a break.* "Gee, thanks. I'll save your recipes, maybe get you some money in the process, and I'll still be in a scummy profession."

"I didn't say that. You know me. I was just quoting." Rachel reached for her coat, her sobbing fit concluded. Back in place was the strong woman of action who refused to be defeated. The pity party was over. Colin would not see her as a weakling again.

"By the way, that wasn't what Shakespeare meant. You used the words out of context. Characters in the play were trying to plan a rebellion and figured they needed to take down the legal system to do it. You and your quotations." Colin grinned. "It's good to know some things haven't changed. Do you remember that night we had the champagne? I've never had anyone spout as many quotations in my ear as you did. That's how I knew you were tipsy."

"I was young. It didn't take much alcohol to make me drunk," Rachel said brusquely. They'd kissed, and now was not the time to rehash how memorable that had been—not. "I'm no longer a lightweight. One thing about working at an Italian restaurant, I drank a lot of wine."

"Maybe we'll have to discover what type of stuff you're made of one night when neither of us is driving," Colin said. His phone rang, and he picked it up and listened to his paralegal. "Just have her hold for a moment. I'm wrapping up now."

Rachel couldn't help herself. "Girlfriend?"

"Client," Colin said. He shot her a wicked grin. "Why? Interested?"

She shrugged, cool and composed. "Only for the sake of having some fresh gossip to toss about the diner. It might take everyone's attention off me."

"Ah." He nodded, as if not buying her explanation in the slightest. "I'll stop by tomorrow and let you know about fees. I usually do lunch at Kim's on Thursdays."

"Prime-rib special," Rachel said. "Been that way every week for at least twenty years."

"And I try not to miss it. Tomorrow every seat will be full. Your mom and grandmother serve the best prime rib in town, even better than the stuff at the Sherman House in Batesville, and that's fantastic. Do you want me to walk you out?"

She turned her head to ascertain if he was serious. She was used to walking the streets of New York at night. She could handle small-town Morrisville, one of the safest places on the planet. "No," she said. "I'm not that bad off. Attend to your call. I can find the way."

He sent her an appreciative smile. "Great. Then I'll see you tomorrow."

She'd just reached the door, when his voice had her glancing around. "Rachel?"

He held the phone, his hand covering the mouthpiece. "Yes?" she said.

"In case I forget to tell you this later, it's good to have

you back. And don't worry, we'll get him." He stood there at his desk, impeccable in his blue broadcloth shirt, matching tie and dress pants.

"Don't keep your caller waiting," she chided, trying to tame her racing heart. She tugged her purse strap higher on her shoulder.

She did not need to start entertaining any silly notions about Colin. Her time in Morrisville was temporary. Not a life sentence. Just a quick hit before she went back to New York, even if she had to stay the full six months before her noncompete clause expired. She gave Colin one last glance. He was silhouetted against the windows, a man secure in his element and this small provincial town.

One she'd left long ago.

Chapter Three

"Hi, honey. I'm glad you're here," Colin's mother, Loretta, said when he arrived at his parents' place later that evening. She accepted the kiss he planted on her cheek. "Your father's in the library. Dinner will be ready in about twenty-five minutes. Kristin's bringing the twins. She's running about ten minutes late."

"Is Jack working?" Colin asked. His older sister's husband was a psychologist. They had two seven-year-old identical twin girls, who, while adorable, were a handful.

"He's got patients scheduled until nine, I think Kristin said. Now, shoo. No men here in the kitchen while I cook."

Colin snagged a crouton from atop a plate of salad and laughed as he left the enormous kitchen, remodeled long ago. His mother loved to cook and her pantry was the size of a bedroom, and she kept it well stocked. When Colin and his three sisters had all lived at home, his mother had fed them and their friends.

She still fed her family, which now included spouses and a horde of grandchildren that multiplied every year. This time it was older sister Amanda who was incubating baby number three. His other sister, Anne Louise, already had four kids. She'd had one boy, then a set of twins and then another girl, who'd turned two in June. Her husband was currently Indiana's junior senator, and they were talking a total of six. Colin had always told his younger sister she was nuts, but she'd only laughed at him and told him to get a life.

Besides get-togethers, his mother cooked every year for the Morris family annual Thanksgiving celebration, which had over thirty people for the traditional turkey dinner and at least a hundred friends, associates and towns-folk stopping by the house throughout the day. Easter was coming in mid-March this year, and that holiday would be almost as crazy. The only difference was that the towns-people wouldn't stop by.

"Hey, Dad," Colin greeted his father, entering the library. Whereas the kitchen was totally a woman's area, the library was a man's room. Reginald and Loretta Morris had always joked that their marriage worked because they kept certain rooms "one sex only." They'd celebrated their thirty-eighth wedding anniversary last year, so Colin figured that whatever household arrangement they had was a good one. He'd never doubted the bond his parents shared.

"Hi, Colin," Reginald said. He lifted his Scotch-and-water in salute. "Shall I pour you one?"

Colin shook his head. "Not tonight." Ever since one of his and Bruce's friends had died during high school, driving under the influence, he and Bruce hardly touched alcohol, especially if either would be behind the wheel later.

"Ah," Reginald said, nodding his understanding. "So tell me, how's the plane search going?"

Colin grinned. When he'd turned eighteen, his parents

had given him a present of six flying lessons. The hobby had stuck. "We found one we like and we're buying it."

Reginald tapped a forefinger on the glass. "Really?"

Colin's grin widened. It wasn't every day your son announced he was buying a half-million-dollar Cessna with a group of friends. "Yeah. We're drawing up the legal contracts now as to shares, usage, payments, insurance, etcetera. We'll keep the plane at the airport here."

The Morrisville Airport was unmanned and uncontrolled. Colin had learned to fly at a regional airport with a control tower, but he'd become adept at flying in and out of an airport without towers.

"Your mother won't like this," Reginald tried.

"She's finally promised to fly with me—this spring," Colin said. "I'm good, Dad, and I'm safe. It's Bruce who got hurt, remember?"

"Hmph." His father exhaled. In addition to being a lawyer, Bruce had volunteered as a firefighter, until the ceiling of Kim's Diner had collapsed on him. He'd suffered a broken arm but otherwise had been fine. He'd retired from the fire department right after the accident and married Christina. Colin had never had the urge to fight fires. Instead, his rush came from piloting. He could remember his first solo as if it were yesterday.

Sensing now was a good time to change the subject, he said, "I saw Rachel Palladia today."

His father swirled the liquid in his glass. "I heard Rachel broke off with her young man."

Colin glanced out the library window. Night had fallen, and because of the dense trees, he couldn't tell if any lights were on at the Palladia house next door. "That's true. Rachel told me the whole story. Did you hear that he's threatening to sue her for her recipes? Says they belong to him."

"Hadn't heard that part," Reginald said, setting his Scotch down. "What a damn shame. Is that what you and she talked about today?"

"Yeah. She says the recipes came from Kim. Since there's no specific work-for-hire contract regarding her recipes, meaning they didn't have a payment plan for those, I'm pretty convinced he's just bullying her. He's not happy she broke off the engagement and is probably smarting from having to change his menu."

"Maybe he should have kept his pants up," Reginald said sharply. He caught Colin's shocked expression. "What? Told you I knew everything."

"Well…" Colin felt embarrassed. Sometimes being man-to-man with your dad was awkward, even if you did work with him. He regained his composure. "I'd like to take on Rachel's case. I told her I'd discuss it with you first. I don't think he'll go as far as a court filing."

"Okay," Reginald said easily. "We've been handling the Palladia family's legal matters for years. Adding Rachel as a client is only logical."

"There's one little catch." Colin paused and rubbed the back of his neck. "Rachel doesn't have a lot of money. She says she's pretty close to broke, which is why she's back living at home."

"I'd heard that, too," Reginald said. "Kim told me Rachel won't accept anything from either her mother or grandmother. Kim offered her an outrageous salary and Rachel said no. She's a Palladia, all right. Take nothing from anybody if you don't know you can repay it."

Colin's chin itched and he scratched the stubble. His

five-o'clock shadow was arriving. "Could I lower my hourly rate for her? Do some of her case pro bono? You're always saying the firm should do more of that, give back to the community."

Reginald paced for a minute. "I'd have to discuss this with the partners, but as longtime clients, I don't foresee a problem waiving some billable hours."

Colin poured himself a glass of water from the small bar sink. "I told her I'd go over at lunchtime tomorrow and let her know."

"Then I'll work on getting an answer first thing in the day and give it to you by noon. I'm not missing prime rib, either."

"Great. I can put in something myself, if that helps," Colin said, meaning taking a cut in salary on this case. His bungalow was almost paid for. His car was paid in full. Except for the really expensive plane he would be a quarter owner of, he didn't have any superhuge monthly bills.

Reginald's eyes narrowed, wrinkling the skin at the corner. "I do have one question before you accept Rachel as a client. Will you be able to maintain your professional objectivity?"

The question caught Colin off guard and his heart seemed to stop. "What do you mean by that?"

Reginald coughed, as was his habit when addressing a delicate matter. "You and Rachel were always good friends. She practically lived over here. She's like a fourth daughter to your mother and me. Since you two were so close, it's natural that you want to rush to her defense and be her knight in shining armor."

Colin stared at his father for a moment, processing his words. He had wanted to throttle her ex this afternoon. But that didn't mean he would be reactive. He and Rachel weren't... Then Colin understood his father's concern.

"Oh, I get it," he said. "You think I… She. No. No, it's not like that. She was always over here because she had a crush on Bruce, not me. If you're like a parent to her, I'm like her brother. She never thought of me as anything else, or as anything more than a buddy."

Reginald arched his left eyebrow. "Even if you did?"

Colin shifted his weight, crossed his arms and simply waited, as if doing so would deny the truth. He'd always liked Rachel, and now a beautiful and intriguing woman had replaced the gangly girl of his childhood.

"Son, it was so obvious to your mother and me that you had the biggest crush on her," Reginald said quietly. "Kim, Rachel's mother—Adrienne—your mother and I would joke that someday the two of you should get married, you were so like peas in a pod. You even finished each other's sentences. We said it would finally unite our families. After all, we've been living next door to each other for generations. Your mother had the whole thing thought out."

Colin sputtered on the water he'd been sipping. "That's morbid."

Reginald waved dismissively. "Oh, it's a thing parents who are friends do. You'll understand someday. You like to pretend you can somehow predestine your child's future. You do it although you know your plans won't come true. You went to college, she went to cooking school, and each of you moved on with your lives. That's just how things go."

Reginald set his empty glass on the side bar. "As much as your mother and I would love for you to settle down, we know you'll do that when the time's right. I just want to be sure you'll be objective in Rachel's case."

Colin forced himself not to cross his arms across his chest after he placed his glass in the sink. "As you said, we've both moved on. She's planning on going back to New York. Her life isn't in Morrisville anymore. And I'm not going to be anyone's rebound guy, so even if she did choose me, which, may I remind you, she never has and won't because she's never thought of me as anything more than a friend, nothing's going to happen. Client relationship only."

"If you're sure," Reginald said. Colin didn't have a chance to further refute his father's doubt, because his sister Kristin arrived and seven-year-old twins bounded in with yells of "Hi, Grandpa! We're here. Can you tell us apart today?" To which Reginald promptly said Libby was the one with the red bow and Maggie was the one with the blue. He was right, of course, and within minutes all had taken their seats at the breakfast-room table, a more comfortable venue than the massive dining-room table, which sat sixteen.

"So, Uncle Colin, will you be there?" Libby asked, and Colin focused on his niece.

"Be there for what?" he asked.

"We're doing a St. Patrick's Day feast at our school. St. Paddy's Day is on Monday this year. We've already started making our leprechaun traps. Anyways, we get to invite someone special. I have to bring cupcakes. They have to be from a bakery. Something about hepa something." Libby said.

"Hepatitis," her sister finished.

"What about your mom and dad?" Colin asked. He didn't want to be usurping anyone's invitation.

"Dad's got patients and Mom's already volunteering, so she doesn't count. I thought I'd bring you. I keep telling my friends you have a plane."

"Not yet," Colin said.

Libby frowned. "But you fly a lot. Remember, you took us up. That wasn't your plane?"

"I rented it," he said. He'd flown both twins and Kristin, providing them an aerial view of the town and their house. Colin smiled. "But that doesn't matter. You name me the dates, and if I'm not required in court, we'll go flying. And I will definitely be at your feast."

"Good." Libby seemed satisfied, and dinner continued. Afterward everyone hung out in the family room for a while before Kristin took the girls home around seven-thirty.

"Hey, Mom, do you still have my high-school yearbook?" Colin asked, walking into the kitchen. "I was looking for it at my place the other day and couldn't find it."

"If I do, it's in your old bedroom," she said. She loaded the plates into the dishwasher.

"You know I would have helped with that," Colin said.

"Yes, but I told you I had it." She straightened. "What do you want your yearbook for?"

"I realized I had the other three but not my senior year's," he said. "Thought I'd just grab it while I was here."

His mom wiped her hands on her apron. "I think it's on your bookshelf."

Colin climbed the back stairs two at a time to the second floor. The house had a third floor, but that was mainly a big playroom that only the grandchildren now used.

His mom had redecorated some of the other rooms, making them more kid friendly for the grandchildren, who stayed over on occasion, but Colin's room remained largely untouched. He'd left behind his old childhood furniture, opting to buy a new king-size bed instead of keeping the twin he'd grown up on. He had removed most of his childhood mementos from the room, although they were stored in a box in his basement instead of holding a place of prominence in his own home.

Since his old room was located on the east side of the house and faced the side yard, he had one four-foot-wide window instead of two or more like many of the Victorians. He flipped the light switch, activating the lamp, and moved toward the bookcase, situated near the window and still lined with high-school and college texts. The shelves also still held aviation magazines, a golf trophy from a charity match and, on the bottom shelf, his yearbook. He leaned down, removed it and straightened. As he did, a flash of light caught his eye. He stood there in the window, clearly in view, before reaching down and turning off the lamp.

Rachel was in her room. He couldn't see her clearly without binoculars, something they'd both used until their teen years. But behind the sheer curtains he could see her silhouette as she stood there, staring across the way— right at him.

When he was a child, none of this was forbidden. He'd take his flashlight, let her know he was there, and they'd send Morse code messages across their yards until one of their parents would discover they were still awake and yell at them to go to sleep. Never once had there been anything sexual about their communication, even when he'd been in high school and realized his feelings for Rachel went beyond friendship.

So why did he have the impression that unlike when they were children, he was somehow a voyeur, a Peeping Tom? And as he saw Rachel lift her arms as if removing a T-shirt, try as he might, he couldn't get his feet to move one inch or his head to turn.

A light flashed across the way, a small circular beam like from a flashlight's. He froze. Had she spotted him? He hadn't been in his room long. He'd turned off the light and was hidden in the darkness and the blinds were only open a sliver. The beam flashed two short, then one long. Then a pause with no light, then one long flash before the light went off again. She'd communicated two letters. *U* then *T.* Their code for *You there?*

She must have seen him moving around earlier. His silhouette certainly didn't match his mother's. If Rachel had watched him walk in, she would have recognized him. Is that why she'd signaled?

His eyes, accustomed to the room's darkness, sought the flashlight that had lived on the bookshelf. His fingers reached for it, but found nothing. His mother might have removed it.

Across the way, Rachel's flashlight had fallen silent. He could use lamplight to answer, but that would illuminate him. They'd never done that to communicate.

His cell phone would have to do. He drew the blinds, flipped the device open and held it open for a long, then short, then two long flashes. The letter *Y.*

Yes. I'm here.

Funny, how easily the knowledge returned. When he'd first learned Morse code, he'd had to glance at a sheet of paper to spell out words. He hadn't used the code in thirteen years, yet the dots and dashes came easily as he and Rachel began to "talk."

What did he say? she asked.

Ninety percent yes, Colin flashed back. *Will know for sure by noon.*

How was dinner? she sent him.

Great. Nieces here. Been invited to a school feast. This is like old times. Fun.

Agreed, she returned.

Colin stood there for a second, trying to figure out what to say next. He was supposed to be a professional, and here he was acting like a child and sending messages with his cell phone's display light. Heck, years ago they hadn't had cell phones. Now he could just dial Rachel up and talk to her that way. But here he remained, in the dark, enjoying the illicit thrill of communicating this way.

"Colin? Are you up there still? Did you find it? Do you need some help?" his mother called.

Colin quickly flashed three letters, *G-T-G,* his and Rachel's code for *Got to go,* which usually indicated one of their parents was about to bust them.

He shoved his phone back in his pocket. He was thirty-one years old, and his mom was about to discover him in his old bedroom, flashing his phone at the girl next door. She wouldn't understand. He grabbed the yearbook off the bed, and as he left his bedroom, he ran into his mother as she rounded the corner. "I found it," he told her, taking four steps down the hall.

"Oh," she said. "I was starting to wonder what was keeping you. I mean, I thought I'd seen your yearbook last on the bookshelf."

"It was in my closet," Colin fibbed, glad he was behind his mother, who'd already turned toward the stairway. He clutched the book to his chest and followed her down into the kitchen. "I've got to get going. It's getting late," he told her.

"Okay," she said. She gave him a quick hug. "Stay safe."

"I will." With that and a quick goodbye to his father, Colin was soon outside and climbing into his sedan. The driveway was on the opposite side of the house from Rachel's window, so he couldn't see if she was still in her bedroom. Once he backed out, a maze of tree branches should block any clear view.

But somehow, he saw her standing in the window as he drove by.

RACHEL SIGHED and set her flashlight down on the bed. Her mother was one of those home-safety types who had flashlights that also served as night-lights plugged into at least one outlet in every bedroom. Rachel had grown up knowing an evacuation plan for fire, tornado and earthquake. Considering that fire had destroyed the diner, maybe her mother's better-safe-than-sorry attitude wasn't so hard to understand.

She glanced around her bedroom. Little had changed since high school. The antique white canopy bed had been in the room for years. The wallpaper was Victorian—faded cabbage-rose wallpaper that had become cream colored with age. Only the white lacy bedspread was new.

Growing up, Rachel had always wanted something more modern. Her apartment decor had leaned toward black and chrome, befitting a New York City studio whose only view was the building next door.

A knock sounded, and her mother entered. Rachel stood five-seven; Adrienne Palladia topped out at five-two. "I brought your laundry," she said.

"You didn't have to do that," Rachel said, rising from where she'd been flopped on the bed.

"It was no problem," her mom insisted, setting the white circular basket on a small, upholstered chair and walking back to the doorway. As she did, she noticed the flashlight on the bedspread. "What's that doing out?"

"Uh…" Rachel stammered.

Her mother frowned. "Were you flashing Colin again? He doesn't even live there anymore."

"Um…" Rachel fought to think of something plausible. Although she'd never told Colin, on a long-ago visit home from New York City she'd confessed her nocturnal childhood activities. "I was just trying to see if I could peer into his room the way I used to do. Call it curiosity. I saw him today when I went to catch Bruce."

That was safe and reasonable.

"You saw Colin?" Her mother had moved to the doorway and she paused.

"Yes, he was walking into the law office as I was walking out. He asked me what I was doing there, so I told him. Bruce is in Houston with Christina."

"And…" her mother prompted.

"He'll let me know tomorrow if Lancaster and Morris will take on my case. He's meeting me at the diner around noon."

"Then I'll keep my fingers crossed for good news. I hope it all works out, especially since you won't let us help you."

Rachel shook her head. "You and Grandma are already doing enough, although there is one thing I want to talk about with both of you. I'd like to maybe use the kitchen."

Adrienne's brow creased, as if she was confused about why her daughter would ask a question with such an obvious answer. "Of course you can. This house is too big for the three of us, but it's been in the family forever. Who knows, maybe one of these days I'll move in with you the way Kim did with me."

"I guess you're lucky that you get along so well with Dad's mother." Marco's mother had accepted Rachel, but she hadn't been overly friendly.

"We're best friends," Adrienne said, and Rachel knew her mother meant it. "I'm closer to her than I was to my mom, God rest her soul."

Rachel smiled. One of her mother's foibles was to add *God rest her soul* when speaking of the dead, as if not doing so might bring someone back to haunt her. "Amen," Rachel quipped. "But back to the kitchen. I wasn't talking about here. I'd like to use the one at the diner after it closes. I'd like to begin baking. Maybe fill up the display case in the front. My dream is to get a small Internet bakery business going, although I haven't pursued that yet. This could help me begin. I'll pay you both for the usage."

Her mom leaned her hip against the doorjamb. "If you're a little strapped for cash, we could do an exchange. You give us some desserts to sell during our business hours and I'll give you use of the kitchen. That's probably a fair trade. I doubt Kim will mind."

"Mind what? I'm hearing my name. Is this a meeting?" Kim slid by Adrienne and entered Rachel's bedroom. It always amazed Rachel how thin and spry her grandmother was. Turning seventy hadn't slowed her down at all. Her grandmother still did yoga and tai chi to keep her five-foot-four body flexible.

"Rachel wants to use the diner's kitchen in exchange for giving us some goodies to sell in the front display case," Adrienne said.

"Can you make my bear claws?" Kim said, peering at her granddaughter.

"Actually, yes," Rachel confirmed. "And cakes, pies and other pastries. I thought I'd test some new recipes, and look into what it would take to open a cyber bakery."

"Don't know what the world's coming to." Kim shook

her head in disbelief. "Still don't understand why anyone wouldn't just go to their local store for something fresh baked. Heck, you can get cakes decorated in Wal-Mart and they're quite tasty. The girls at the diner bought me one for my last birthday. Not as good as mine, but not half-bad, either."

"So can she use the kitchen or not?" Adrienne asked, bringing Kim back to the real subject.

Kim nodded. "Of course. It's a great idea. I'm sure you'll have plenty of orders. Closest Wal-Mart is in Greensburg and closest supermarket is in Batesville. The way the price of gas is, if your desserts are any good, you'll be swarmed with buyers."

"I hope so," Rachel said. "I could use the money. This will also give me a chance to develop some new recipes if Marco does end up winning."

"He won't," her mother reassured her. "Rachel saw Colin Morris about Marco's demand letter," she explained to Kim. "He's going to let her know tomorrow whether he can take the case. He probably has to discuss it with the partners."

"If Reginald says no, I'll go next door and give him a piece of my mind. Loretta will let me, too. Either that or I'll add hot-pepper sauce to his prime rib tomorrow."

Rachel laughed. She loved her feisty grandmother. "There won't be any need to poison Mr. Morris. Colin just wanted to discuss fees with him. I'm sure everything will be fine."

"Of course it will. Colin's turning into quite a good lawyer," her mother said.

"Not that anyone but him doubted he would," Kim interjected. "The boy has to believe in himself more. He's always had to play second fiddle to Bruce. Now, that boy was smart. Highest bar score in the state."

"I asked for Bruce, but he's on vacation with his wife," Rachel said.

"Oh, she's a pretty thing, too," Kim said. "I told you that story already, right?"

"Yes," Rachel said. Kim knew everything that went down in Morrisville.

"I'm sure Colin will do a good job on your case," Adrienne said.

Kim blinked rapidly—she was still all fired up. "Why wouldn't he? Heck, you'll probably get more personal attention having Colin as your lawyer. That boy had a crush on you for years. And you certainly didn't turn into an ugly duckling in New York."

"What?" Rachel asked, not sure she'd heard her grandmother correctly.

"I said you didn't get ugly when you moved to New York," Kim replied, shifting her weight.

"No, before that. That Colin had a crush on me," Rachel said.

"He did," Kim replied with a nod. "We all thought you had to be crazy to pass him by."

We? Who was we? Unsettled, Rachel probed on a different front. "He didn't have a crush on me. Remember? Prom? I told you, he didn't ask me. I just heard him wrong. He went with someone else."

"I thought *you* turned *him* down. You know, you two really should discuss that," Adrienne said. "Get it out in the open and put it behind you."

"It is behind me," Rachel argued, realizing that the moment she'd stepped foot in Morrisville her past had roared to life. In New York, Colin Morris had been her previous life. All women had some man who broke their hearts, intentionally or not. It was simply a rite of passage, a part of growing up. Now she was face-to-face with him, and the truth was, he hadn't ever liked her as more than a friend, no matter how deep her feelings for him.

That he might have fallen in love with her had been a wild fantasy of hers, and a terribly misguided one at that. She'd learned of her mistake the hard way. "Besides, whatever he might have felt, that was high school. Years ago. Way too long to worry about now. And remember Marco? I believed I was getting married. It's not even been three weeks."

"Colin's never been serious about anyone," Kim announced, ignoring the proclamation about Marco, whom she'd never liked in the first place, especially when he'd tried to talk to her about the Old Country the one time they'd met.

"I was committed and I don't want to get involved on the rebound. I have no intention of just finding some other man to keep my bed warm."

Her mother crossed herself and Rachel rolled her eyes. Her mother had been a virgin until she'd married. She also still went to church every Sunday and didn't miss a holy day. Compared with her, Rachel was quite the heathen. "Sorry," she mumbled.

"Oh, lighten up, Adrienne. You know how kids these days are," Kim said. "Rachel's a grown woman. You married at twenty. I'd be worried about her if she hadn't, well…"

"I just don't want to hear the details," Adrienne said. "Feel free to use the kitchen. We usually finish the next day's prep work around five. It's yours after that."

"Thanks," Rachel said. "The arrangement is only temporary, though. My goal has always been to open a place in New York and sell on the Internet from it. I love the vibes of the city. But I can't tell you enough how much I appreciate your support. I'm very lucky."

"Sweetie, you're family. This is what family does. We only wish you'd let us do more to help you," Adrienne said.

"What you've done is plenty," Rachel insisted. She stood and hugged them. "I love you both dearly."

"Us, too," Kim said.

Another round of hugs followed, and then Rachel found herself alone again. She glanced at the clock. Kim and Adrienne opened the diner by 6:00 a.m. so they were usually in bed by eight. Since tomorrow Rachel's shift didn't start until eleven, she could sleep in a little if she wanted. Not that she was tired. She was still on edge from finding Colin Morris in his darkened bedroom, flashing code back at her.

What had made her grab the flashlight and contact him when she'd seen the light go on in his bedroom? She'd instinctively known it was him, and no one else. She sprawled out on her back and stared up at the double bed's lace canopy. She had to be the world's biggest idiot. Not only had she not suspected Marco's indiscretions, but she'd just acted like a middle-school girl with a crush—on a man who only wanted to help her with her legal issues.

Which he was doing because she was a friend, or like his sister. Nothing more. She'd clear up any misconceptions tomorrow. If not, the people in this small town would get the wrong idea and start pairing her with Colin. That would be bad, especially since her stay was temporary.

Besides, she didn't like him in a romantic sense. Maybe she had long ago. But now, not one bit. Although she *had* just flashed him messages across the night. Chalk that up to being one of the many mistakes she'd made with Colin Morris. Well, no more. She'd make it perfectly plain they were going to keep everything professional. She'd straighten out this crush nonsense. Tomorrow, they'd clear the air.

Chapter Four

By ten minutes to noon, Rachel was a basket case. She'd never been so nervous. She wiped her palms on her chef's jacket, smearing the white icing that had attached itself to her fingers.

It probably didn't help her psyche, either, that she hadn't slept well. She'd read a book until almost midnight because she'd had insomnia. Then, when she'd finally fallen asleep, just about every dream had been of Colin Morris. They'd been children in one, playing down at the creek. They'd been high schoolers in another, dancing cheek to cheek at the prom they'd never attended. The last dream had been the most erotic, and Rachel blushed, thinking of what she'd done in that one.

She grabbed a tray of pastries, used her hip to push open the kitchen door and carried the tray out to the display case by the cash register. She was putting out the various pastries her grandmother had baked. Within two days, Rachel planned to have everything in the display case be her own wares.

She busied herself with setting everything inside, bending over to rearrange the pumpkin bread she'd placed there at eleven. Already, half of it had been sold.

Her mind drifted back to the last dream, the one that still

haunted her. In it, Colin had looked exactly as he had in his office—minus all his clothes. And she and Colin hadn't been in his office but in a bedroom, on a bed. Naked and intertwined.

She'd woken up in a hot sweat, breathing heavily. So much for not liking the man. If her very realistic dream was any indication, she wanted to jump him. She was interested in him, at least sexually. Not good. She had to get those lustful urges behind her.

Rachel completed reorganizing the same moment legs clad in expensive suit pants suddenly appeared in front of the display case. She pulled back slowly, careful not to whack her head on the top of the case.

The object of last night's lust stood there, a grin covering his face and immediately sending shivers throughout her body. Last night she'd kissed him. Sure, only in her subconscious, but having the flesh-and-blood Colin standing a mere countertop away was throwing her equilibrium off in a manner she had never experienced.

"Hi," he said.

"Hey," Rachel said, ignoring her grandmother's pointed interest even though she was ringing up a customer. "Kim's busy, so I can seat you. Will anyone be joining you?" Rachel reached for the menus.

He shook his head. "Actually, I know I said we'd talk, but the judge has made his decision on one of my cases, and I have to run over to the courthouse." Colin glanced around the diner, which was packed with the noontime prime-rib-craving lunch crowd. Rachel followed his gaze, recognizing most of the diners as locals who came and ate here a couple of times a week. "I phoned in and have a take-out order. Do you have a minute?"

"I guess." Not that there was anywhere private at Kim's to talk.

Colin seemed to sense this, as well. He hesitated. "I won't be finished with the paperwork until about four today. Could we meet for dinner? I'd like to discuss your matter further. The partners met and we're taking you on as a client."

Relief swept over Rachel, vanquishing the apprehension she'd felt when Colin had mentioned dinner. This wasn't a date. Just a lawyer-client thing.

Although, did lawyers invite their clients to dinner?

"Rachel, you're needed in the kitchen. Your timer went off," Adrienne called. The swinging door closed behind her.

"I've got to go," Rachel said.

"How about I pick you up at five?" Colin proposed.

"I can meet you," she replied as Kim put a white carry-out sack in front of Colin.

"I'll pick you up. It's not a problem. I know where you live," Colin said. "Kim, put this on my tab, will you?"

"Already done," Kim said.

"Thanks." Colin lifted the bag and left, the jingling bell on the door signaling his departure.

Rachel exhaled the breath she hadn't realized she was holding, something her grandmother immediately noticed.

"He looks good in a suit, doesn't he?" Kim mused as she reached for a customer's ticket.

"He's just a friend."

"Uh-huh." Kim smiled at the elderly gentleman. "Was everything okay?"

"Perfect," the man said. "Never tried it here before."

"Well, I hope you come back," Kim said, taking the money he offered and getting his change.

"I'm sure I will," the man promised, and Rachel used

the moment to escape into the kitchen. Colin Morris had looked superb. Regal, in a sense. Naked or suited, he should be outlawed. Locked away out of her sight and forbidden from being in her fantasies. She reached for a cooling loaf pan and turned out the banana bread onto a wire rack.

She'd planned on baking tonight and now she was going to dinner, instead. She calmed her heart, told herself she was being silly. Her goal was to get back to New York, so Colin's legal advice took precedence. She was not going to let him get under her skin.

COLIN WAS PROMPT. She'd watched him drive up at exactly 5:00 p.m. and met him on the porch steps. "What," he said, grinning at her as he exited the car. "Don't even tell me you thought I was going to be late."

She arched an eyebrow at him. The Colin of yesterday hadn't been known for his promptness. He also hadn't been known for driving anything four-door, and probably would have died before owning the sensible gray Saturn Aura in front of her.

"Yes, it's mine," he said, reading her mind. "It's practical—but still sporty."

"Of course it is" she said. The car screamed, *I am now in my thirties and willing to grow up.*

"But not willing to sacrifice," Colin said, holding the door open. He laughed. "I know that's exactly what you were thinking. You had me pegged for some low-slung, two-seater sports car. Well, everything I drive has to have four seats and must be able to fit at least two bags of golf clubs."

"Still playing?"

"As often as I can, although not as much as I'd like," Colin said. "Pretty busy with work lately. I figure this is my year to make full partner, especially at the rate I'm going. The latter part of last year wasn't too shabby."

"So you aren't a full partner yet?" Colin was family; Rachel had expected him to be a shoo-in.

He shut the door and she leaned back against the leather upholstery. The car wasn't new, but it still smelled that way.

Colin climbed in and fired up the engine. "Nope, not yet. Christina was hired as a full partner and that was before Bruce even got his promotion."

They drove down the long, tree-lined street, which seemed so much smaller now that they were no longer children racing Big Wheels or bicycles. Now that spring was right around the corner, it was finally starting to make its presence known. They had a couple more weeks before the leaves popped, but winter was definitely on the way out. Daylight savings time would also begin soon. Rachel smiled. Living in New York, she'd gotten used to "springing forward." Her mother hadn't quite adjusted; the state of Indiana had only started setting clocks forward one hour in the spring a few years ago.

"So where are we going?" Rachel asked, lowering the visor. With the days growing longer, the sun was still above the horizon and wouldn't dip below for about another hour, give or take a minute or two.

"To the River Club," Colin said. He turned down a narrow two-lane road and headed toward the outskirts of town.

"Never heard of it," Rachel said. Morrisville wasn't known for its culinary delights. In fact, since Kim's closed at three, many people ate dinner at the public golf-course restaurant or at the hospital cafeteria in Batesville. Both were considered fine dining. Rachel gave an involuntary shudder. She'd once agreed, until she'd moved to Manhattan and learned how provincial her life had been.

"Cold?" Colin asked, seeing her second shiver.

"No, I'm fine." Her outfit wasn't the problem. She'd worn black slacks, boots and a red V-neck sweater. The day had been warm, but the air would cool down around seven so she'd brought a field coat. She'd just have to trust Colin's judgment in choosing dining establishments.

They were about ten miles outside of town now, and Rachel frowned. "Why are we at the airport? Did they reopen the café?"

The airport had had a small diner, but the owners had sold everything, retired and moved to Florida a few years back.

"No," Colin said.

He was being deliberately evasive. "We're eating here?" she prodded.

"Nope." He parked his car outside a single-story brick building. A sign, like the cheap kind you find at any hardware store, proudly proclaimed Office. Another sign, on a door about ten feet to the left, proclaimed Lounge. The café building had been demolished, replaced with an airplane hangar.

"Uh, I don't get it," Rachel said, glancing around. The place was pretty quiet, save from the whirring of a power tool in an airport hangar about a hundred feet to her left.

Colin opened his trunk and withdrew a black duffel.

"We're picnicking?" He'd really lost her, and she wasn't one who usually found herself in the dark.

He shook his head. "No. I told you we're eating at the River Club. Our reservation is for seven. Come on. Our transportation is right over there."

He pointed to where a blue-and-white plane sat parked near a few others.

"We're flying? In that?" The smallest aircraft she'd ever

flown in was one of those regional jets that sat fifty. She'd clutched her seat the entire uncomfortable and bumpy flight.

Colin grinned. "Yeah, that's our plane. Isn't it great? It's a Cessna 182. Three hundred horsepower. You'll love it. These seats are more comfortable than those in commercial first class. Besides, how else did you think we'd get to Chicago?"

"Chicago?"

"That's where the River Club is," Colin said.

She looked around, searching for someone—anyone— who could tell her she'd entered the twilight zone. But Colin was already striding over to the plane as if he knew what he was doing. He opened the left-side door, set the duffel on the seat and removed some headphones and his cell, before following with various charts and spiral-bound books. Then he zipped the bag, opened a door in the tail and put the bag inside. "If you want, you can put your purse back here. Or you can stow it at your feet. Your choice. Climb in. You're in the front right seat. I had them gas up the plane already, but I've still got to run the standard takeoff checks."

"Okay," Rachel said. She glanced up and down the airport runway, preferring to stay outside. She set her purse next to his bag after taking a moment to shut off her cell phone. Colin seemed to be everywhere at once, doing what he told her were preflight checks. "So where's the pilot? Shouldn't he be doing this?" she finally asked, although really, part of her already knew the answer.

Colin finished checking their fuel capacity from the top of the plane and he hopped down onto the concrete. "He *is* doing this."

Rachel's jaw dropped. "So you're really flying us in this."

"Yep. I use this baby all the time. Remember Mike

Mertz from high school? Four of us, Mike included, just bought one similar to this, only a year newer. We'll take delivery next month."

She'd heard rumors. Maybe her mother had told her, but Rachel hadn't really believed any of it. Colin wasn't committed enough to anything. Flying required tons of devotion, flight time. It wasn't like golf, where you whacked a little ball around the green and hoped for the best. Even she could do that. "So you have your pilot's license."

"I first soloed right after I turned nineteen. I began before my freshman year of college. My first six were a graduation present. When I got to Indiana University I found the nearest airfield, got a part-time job and started lessons."

"I heard you partied all through college," Rachel said.

"I wasn't a saint," Colin replied. He walked around the airplane and opened the passenger-side door. "Okay, have to give you the spiel. In the event of an emergency, lift up on the silver handle and push outward. Meet by the tail of the plane after we stop."

"You aren't making me feel very safe."

"This plane is one of the safest in the air, and I don't take unnecessary risks. Climb in," he said.

Rachel entered the aircraft and settled into her seat. He was right; it was comfortable. "There's a steering wheel."

"Actually, it's called a yoke. The plane has an all-glass cockpit, too." He gestured to the blank screens below the front windshield. "You'll see all those instruments light up in a few minutes."

Colin shut the door behind her and she secured her seat belt. He slid in next to her, grabbed a binder and began to go through the takeoff checklist. "Put your headphones on," he advised, and his fingers grazed hers as he handed her the set. "Plug those into the connectors by your cup holders."

The second Rachel had them over her ears, the world became silent. Then she heard Colin's voice. "Can you hear me? Lower your mic in front of your mouth to talk."

"You're loud and clear," Rachel said. She adjusted the headset and soon felt the rumble as the plane's high-performance engine roared.

The cockpit screens flared to life, and with a little bump, the plane coasted forward and soon was out on the runway.

Rachel gripped her seat, her knuckles whitening. "What about a flight plan?"

"Relax," Colin said. "We don't have to file one. We're flying under VFR—visual flight rules. I've checked the weather and it's a beautiful night, with practically no wind. Smooth skies."

And with that, he sped up, eased back the yoke and they were airborne.

So HE'D SERIOUSLY pursued his pilot's license. She caught Colin smiling as he listened to the air-traffic controller. As the ground faded beneath them, he programmed their destination into the autopilot. The computer spoke the word *altitude* as they hit eleven thousand feet and slowly Rachel loosened her grip.

"Pretty, isn't it?" he said.

The sunset off the wing was beautiful—a shimmer of yellow and orange on the horizon.

"You should have told me. I could have brought a camera."

He laughed. "If I'd told you, you wouldn't have come. You'd have been too chicken."

"Would not have," she lied.

"Admit it. Only the fact that it was a long walk home and you haven't eaten in a New York-caliber restaurant in a while enticed you to climb aboard."

"Okay, fine. I've been a little deprived lately," she agreed.

"This place will soothe your taste buds. You'll like the River Club. It's one of my favorite places."

Rachel wondered how many other dates he'd taken there, and then chided herself that she was *not* on a date with Colin. Maybe he simply needed the flying hours. She'd heard that pilots had to log so many per month in order to maintain their license.

She listened for a moment to the air-traffic chatter over her headphones. Colin answered some question Rachel didn't understand, and she lowered her microphone and turned her head to gaze out the window. She had some questions of her own, but she didn't want to interrupt his conversation.

There was something about the hum of the engine, and as the flight continued, Rachel relaxed. They were cruising at two hundred miles per hour. Until the sun had gone down, she'd been able to make out the geography below. Now she could only make out the lights. She saw a lone car on the two-lane road. The lights of a lamp on a lakeshore beamed upward. She closed her eyes, the music from the satellite-radio channel a lullaby to her ears. As a child she'd always fallen asleep in the back of her grandfather's big diesel pickup. This was like that and she let the motion soothe her.

She awoke a bit later.

"You were out for fifteen minutes," Colin said.

"I'm sorry," she replied, using her fingers to adjust her microphone. It was strange hearing her voice through the headphones, stranger still to think that she'd dozed off in the first place. She never slept on flights, and once, she'd been up twenty-four hours straight, unable to sleep on the red-eye she'd taken. She'd been the only one awake and reading, her overhead light a tiny beacon in a 767 awash in darkness. She'd never made the mistake of flying late at night again. She'd looked like a zombie for two days as she'd tried to recover.

"We're about twenty minutes from the outskirts of Chicago," Colin announced. "We're approaching from the south. You probably can't see it, but Lake Michigan is underneath us."

"Is that why the radio chatter has increased?" She'd been listening to all sorts of conversation, including one that Colin answered. Then he'd adjusted his altitude, dropping a thousand feet.

"We're on Chicago approach. Air-traffic control is watching everything, including us. We're a target on the screen."

"It's fascinating." The monitor in front of her was all lit. Colin explained how one screen showed her the horizon and how Colin's plane was in level flight. The other screen displayed the terrain, weather and other traffic around Colin's plane.

"It's sort of like boating, isn't it, only in three dimensions," Rachel noted at the end of his explanation.

"Yep. We've got a 757 about two thousand feet above us."

"It's fascinating," she breathed. The terrain underneath them had gone from dark farmland or lake water to suburbia awash in twinkling lights.

"Not going to ignore you, but as I'm hungry, let's get this on the ground."

For the next few minutes Colin routed the plane around

Chicago, the turn showing as a fifteen-degree angle on the screen in front. Colin had several conversations with the control tower, and the plane descended. "Get ready. We're on final approach."

Rachel gripped her seat, and amazingly the metal bird drifted down and landed with a light *thunk*. Unlike the heavier commercial planes, the touchdown was gentle and the braking swift. Colin made a right turn off the runway and began his taxi to an aviation hangar. Rachel watched as Colin followed the hand signals of the line guy, parked the plane and shut down the engine.

"Okay, you can remove your headphones. We're here at Chicago Midway."

Rachel took them off and immediately ran her fingers through her hair in an attempt to straighten the brown strands. Colin was already out of the plane and coming around to her side.

"The car's waiting," he announced as he opened her door. He held his hand out to assist her, and she grasped it as she ventured out onto the step molded into the plane's side. She was so intent on the black Lincoln town car parked on the tarmac that she didn't remember there was a large wing overhead. She straightened and banged the top of her head on the underside of it.

"Careful." Colin steadied her, his touch on her arm soft yet firm. "Are you okay?"

She had both feet on the ground, and her head throbbed from the thump. Mere inches separated their bodies and his free hand had moved up to feel her head, his fingers sliding through her hair, searching for a bump. They were friends. They'd yanked on each other's arms when someone was excited, tugged on each other's clothes to make someone change direction, reached for each other's hands when climbing trees and crawling through tunnels.

He'd never touched her like this that she could recall. Maybe he had, but only in sympathy. For the loss of her dog.

"I'm fine," she managed to say. "Nothing some acetaminophen won't fix, and I've got some tablets in my purse."

He still didn't move his hand, his fingertips massaging the sore spot. Two acetaminophen caplets would cut the pain, but nothing would put out the fire zinging in her veins.

The touch was too intimate. She ducked her head and took two steps toward the car. "Will you pass me my purse and coat?"

They didn't touch as he handed her both items. The limo driver climbed from the Lincoln, his posture anticipatory. Colin gestured. "Go ahead. I'll be right there. I have to lock up."

Within a few minutes they were both seated in the back of the town car, and soon they were at the River Club, a three-year-old establishment located high above the Chicago River. The restaurant catered to a casual yet upscale clientele, and Rachel and Colin's table afforded them a fantastic view of the river, the downtown skyline and Lake Michigan.

"So, how is it?" Colin asked much later in the evening, a few minutes after their entrées arrived.

Rachel finished swallowing the delicious bite of salmon. "You did good," she said, smiling. "I love Kim's, but this is why I left Morrisville. Real food. In fact, so far the entire night has been great. How'd you find this place?"

"Another pilot recommended it."

"Your own culinary network," she observed.

He grinned and ate some of his steak. "Exactly. We call it going out for the five-hundred-dollar hamburger."

Understanding he meant the cost of fuel and plane rental for the trip, Rachel felt humbled. "You didn't have to fly me to dinner."

He shrugged. "I wanted to. I love to fly, and try to be in the air at least six hours a week. It's my great escape."

"I don't think I ever would have believed it," Rachel admitted.

"Well, Bruce wanted to be a firefighter. I wanted to be a pilot. We each got what we wanted, sort of."

"Morris and Lancaster boys are lawyers," Rachel finished. "But didn't Bruce quit volunteering?"

"Only after he was injured and Christina came along. Although I doubt I'll have to stop flying. Anyway, I've often wondered if my children will feel that type of pressure. Should I ever have children," Colin added quickly. "I mean, I really don't think about children much. Christina's pregnant, though, and Bruce is already over the top."

He appeared flustered, and Rachel laughed and touched his arm. "I understand what you mean. I grew up an only child. Your place was a madhouse with all those siblings and their friends."

"My mom liked having kids. She's thrilled to be a grandmother. My sisters have kept her in good supply, although she keeps saying she's ready for more. Twins run in my family so maybe she'll get her wish."

"Why haven't you gotten married?"

"Same reason as you?" Colin said, his tone indicating he was uneasy with the question.

Rachel leaned back in her chair. "I hope your fiancée doesn't cheat on you."

He shook his head, aghast at his blunder. "Sorry. Shouldn't have reminded you."

Rachel put her fork on her plate, temporarily full. "No, it's okay. The thought's getting easier to deal with. The biggest blow was to my ego. I mean, I wasn't good enough. Do you know how hard that is?"

Colin bent his head to take a bite of steak. "Actually, yes," he admitted.

Rachel didn't believe him. "Oh, I don't buy that. Women flocked to you. You had to fight them off."

"Not everyone," Colin said testily. He shoved a forkful of food into his mouth.

"Still," Rachel said, watching him chew, "you're a local boy. A good catch. I'm surprised no one has snagged you."

"You make it sound so simple," Colin said after he swallowed. "As if I'm just an item on a grocery store shelf."

"Well, I would have," Rachel said. Might as well get started if she was going to clear the air once and for all.

He stared at her. "What?"

"I would have taken you home. Some girl is insane to have let you slip through her fingers." She paused for a moment, contemplating her next line. "You didn't dump all of them, did you?"

Colin managed to smile. "No. Some of the dissolutions were mutual. Others, I have to admit, *I* broke off. They got too clingy. I want to marry for love, not because it's...well, whatever it's called. Biological clock? Do guys even have those?"

"Marco did, so it's probably wise you recognized you might have one," Rachel said. "Love is the ideal, I think."

"So how did you hook up with him?"

She frowned. "Marco? I worked at his restaurant. He's

very Italian. That was part of the allure. That alpha-male dominance. Someone determined to provide for me. He's a throwback. I realize now it was all an act, but boy, his attention felt good. Here I was, Rachel Nobody, but when I was with Marco, everyone noticed. I didn't realize I was the perfect arm ornament, the ideal wife candidate. Love had nothing to do with it, I recognize that now."

Colin said nothing, letting her finish.

"You asked me once what he saw in me. I've been contemplating that myself. I'm a bit Italian. I'm also a chef, with a diploma from a prestigious culinary school, but I'm not any type of high society. His mother came around a lot and she approved of me for some reason. Maybe Marco simply figured it was time to get married, and since his mother accepted me, I'd do. He actively pursued me. The chase was the fun part."

"It shouldn't be," Colin said. He took a long drink of his club soda. He'd forgone wine because he was the pilot, but had insisted Rachel have a glass. "I've always felt that when you get to the end of the race, you shouldn't find out you don't really want what you've won."

"I guess that's what happened to me," Rachel said. "On his part, at least. I was blissfully planning a wedding. I thought his lack of interest was simply—this sounds cheesy—that he was a guy. He always said weddings were women's work, that I could have whatever I wanted. I lost myself in the fantasy. Got caught up in the moment. Confused being busy with being in love. Thankfully I found out before the wedding. I can't—well, yes, I can—imagine what might have happened a few years down the road."

"I'm sorry," Colin said. He touched her hand, but Rachel snatched it away and held it up, palm out like a shield.

"Don't," she said. "I don't want pity. I've had enough of that. Everyone gives me these glances. I can tell what they're thinking. 'Oh, poor Rachel. If only she'd noticed the signs.' 'Perhaps if she were better in bed, he wouldn't have strayed.' 'Poor thing. She must be reeling.' So please, don't give me any of your pity. Just tell me we're going to kick his…" She checked her language. "His you-know-what. I refuse to lose my recipes."

"And we're going to make sure you don't. Here's what I've decided to do." As they finished their meal, Colin outlined the legal strategy. "I'll be sending out the first letter to his counsel tomorrow. I'll mail you a copy at your house."

"Shouldn't I see it first?"

"You can, but it's all in legalese. You'll have to trust me. I know that's hard, but I have a good feeling about this. You just hang in there. It'll just take time."

The waiter came by with the dessert tray, and Rachel leaned back against her chair, almost defeated. Time was something she seemed to have plenty of lately.

"Would you like to hear about tonight's offerings?" the waiter asked.

"Yes," Colin said. His gaze sought hers. "I'd like something. Rachel?" He pointed to the tray. "The flan here is delicious. Or you could pick something else."

The waiter began to describe the selections, and Rachel succumbed and chose a slice of chocolate cake that appeared positively delicious.

"I'll return with your desserts in a moment," the waiter said, carrying the tray aloft and heading for the kitchen.

"The chocolate cake's a great choice," Colin said.

"Since you ordered the flan, I figured I could always swipe a taste of yours," she said. They used to do that as kids. She'd get the chocolate ice cream; Colin, the vanilla or butterscotch. They'd swap cones back and forth until nothing was left.

"I'll be happy to share if you do the same," Colin replied, his blue eyes darkening, as if he remembered, as well.

"Of course. Although it's hard to even look at someone else's dessert right now," Rachel said.

"Think of it as research," Colin advised, rationalizing.

She nodded. "That's probably a good approach. I start baking all the desserts at Kim's tomorrow afternoon. First up are the pies my grandmother says she's tired of cooking."

"She has been making them for years."

"For as long as I've been alive, and even before that," Rachel acknowledged as she lifted her coffee cup. "I'm ready for the challenge. Hopefully, no one will notice that I'll be tweaking the recipes. She's still making her crusts with lard. It gives the pastry a flakier crust, but it's not good for the arteries. While I was in New York, I created a crust that's just as light and intensely flavorful, but a lot healthier."

Colin rolled his shoulders as if stretching. He noticed her concerned look. "Flying always has my back tightening a little. You shouldn't worry about modifying the pie crust. I doubt anyone will notice you've made any changes. Morrisville's not known for its taste buds."

He'd said the wrong thing, and Rachel's face scrunched up involuntarily as she bit back tears. "I put my foot in my mouth. I mean—" he began.

She shook her head, stopping his explanation. "No, it's okay. Unfortunately, you're absolutely right. Elmer's a prime example. He eats a slice of peach pie a day, but he wouldn't notice the crust unless there wasn't one. Harold's the same way. The only person who really cares about things tasting spectacular is me. I'm the one who wants things five-star in a two-star town."

"I'm not sure if I agree that Morrisville is a two-star town. There are some good things about it, but perhaps not once you've lived in the big city." He toyed with her fingers. "You shouldn't feel guilty for caring about how things taste. Cooking is your passion. You should always strive to be the best. That's what I aim for when I stand up in court and argue for justice, even when it was something as silly as defending Judd after his dog dug up Mrs. Perkins's prize rose beds."

"She always was persnickety over her flowers. I hope it worked out okay."

"It did. She'd taken Judd to small claims to teach him a lesson. Once he offered to help her replant and put in an electric fence, all was well."

Rachel frowned, her own situation weighing heavily on her mind. Her legal situation was "big-time," not small town.

"We will win this," Colin said, as if sensing her mood. "I don't think Marco has a legal precedent to stand on. When he realizes the effort's not worth it, he'll back down and drop the silliness."

"And then I can go back to New York."

Chapter Five

As Rachel made her declaration, she removed her hand out of Colin's reach and broke the connection between them.

"Sure," Colin said, oddly discomfited by her avowal. The waiter brought the flan, but suddenly Colin didn't feel much like eating it, despite the caramelized sugar on the top of the custard. Rachel had only been home since the last week of February, and he wasn't ready to lose her so soon. "You're not planning on staying?"

Rachel shook her head. "Never was. Morrisville is where I'm from. New York is where I want to be. It has such energy. I love it there."

"I'd find it too gray," Colin said.

She nodded. "Oh, it is, but I don't mind. Sure, on overcast winter days, you wonder where the sun is. But the skyscrapers cast interesting long shadows. My apartment window looks across a street and right into someone else's. We have to keep the blinds shut when we get dressed or we'd flash each other, and I'm not really into that stuff. There's always such energy."

"I'd rather have my space," Colin said. "And trees. I can't live without trees."

"Central Park's an easy subway ride away. There are all sorts of other parks around Manhattan. And there's so much to do. Museums. Broadway. Concerts. Great places to eat."

Colin thought she was trying to sell the city a little too hard. "And how often do you get to do those things?"

Her expression tempered. "Not as much as I used to. Marco and I went out frequently, but really, life was pretty much the restaurant every night. However, you have to admit that New York has a lot more cultural and social activities than Morrisville, or even Batesville. What is there to do in Morrisville besides go to the country club? Oh, and Lions, Knights of Columbus, that kind of thing. You have to go to Cincinnati or Indianapolis to find any kind of city life."

"Like I told you, I happen to love playing golf. In fact, one of my favorite things to do when I get the time is load up the clubs, fly to a different city and try a new course. You used to play. Do you still?"

"Not lately, but I'm sure I haven't forgotten," Rachel said defensively.

"Well, maybe you can go a round with me while you're here. Maybe you'll find that it's a sport you might like re-acquainting yourself with."

"I'm sure I'll be baking." Rachel shut the door.

Colin tilted his head and studied her. She squirmed under his scrutiny. "I'm not asking you to go with me as if you were some sort of charity case."

"I just don't want you to get the wrong idea," she replied, jutting her chin defensively.

Colin ate a bite of flan and moved the dessert toward her. "And what wrong idea is that?"

"That I'm wanting anything from you." Rachel helped herself to some of the custard.

"We're friends, aren't we?"

"Yes, but we're no longer children. Morrisville is matchmaking hell. I'm single—you're single. Tongues will wag." She took another bite of the flan. She'd already eaten half the chocolate cake and she pushed that toward him.

"And I'm supposed to worry about that because…?" Colin prompted, reaching for the cake plate.

"Because everyone will try to put one and one together and make two. You and me. That kind of thing."

"Now you're the one trashing my ego," Colin said, forking a morsel, which he raised in the air. "I'm not good enough for you?"

"Of course you are," Rachel said quickly. "In fact, I might have had a teensy crush on you while we were growing up. But I'm not planning on living in Morrisville. You're not planning on leaving. So I'd say, plane or no plane, we're too geographically challenged ever to make anything work. Even if we liked each other, in the future. Not that we will."

He was more interested in her revelation. "You had a crush on me?"

She shoved a bite of flan in her mouth. "Maybe. Just a little one. Nothing much."

Liar. She'd never be able to play poker with him. Still, had he been wrong all these years? "I thought you liked Bruce."

"What?" Her eyes widened. "No. Why would I like him?"

"You were always hanging around him, trying to get his attention," Colin said. He'd set the empty plate to the side.

Rachel appeared discombobulated, which was how he was feeling himself. "I was always hanging around attempting to get *your* attention. You never saw me as anything but the girl next door."

The waiter's arrival with a coffeepot provided an opportune diversion that saved Colin from having to reply. Her declaration was like being blindsided in court.

Rachel had had a crush on him? Impossible. She'd never once given any indication that her feelings ran beyond being a pal.

Perhaps she was toying with him. But the way she was adding cream to her coffee and stirring told him otherwise. "You're about to make a whirlpool and slosh everything over the side."

"Oh." She removed the spoon, stopping the spinning current. "I wasn't paying attention."

"I can see that." Colin chuckled.

She wiggled in her chair. "Well, you've rattled me. This whole return to Morrisville has confounded me. No, my life started changing when I found Marco sleeping with the sous chef. Everything has been topsy-turvy. Nothing seems right anymore."

Her statement gave Colin more insight into how confused Rachel really was. "I'm sorry if I've contributed to your stress," he said finally. He sipped coffee and let the black brew slide down his throat like a bitter balm. "I'm sorry, Rachel. I feel like a cliché. I never meant to cause you any stress or pain."

"Well, you know me. I love clichés and quotes," Rachel quipped, in an attempt to regain her sense of humor. "My goal is to nip any of this tension in the bud. I mean, we cannot go back to high school, when I foolishly adored you. We must keep this relationship professional. Me client—you lawyer. That kind of thing."

"You foolishly adored me?" Colin repeated, using all his skill to keep his myriad emotions from registering on his face. "Rachel, you're killing me here. You liked me that much?"

"Duh," Rachel said. "You men really are clueless. You're perfect proof. We kissed. I thought that meant something. I mean, you asked me to prom, didn't you?"

"Yeah, but I thought you didn't want to go. You never mentioned it the next day. I thought you were embarrassed by what had happened between us."

"Please. It was only a kiss."

"Maybe to you," Colin said. That kiss, with Rachel, whom he'd adored, had been all he'd wanted and more. "It crushed me that you chose to ignore that night and rationalized it away as the consequence of drinking cheap pink champagne."

"Me?" She seemed shocked. "I thought it was all you not wanting to go."

He stared at her, not believing that such a simple thing could spin so far out of control. "I guess we had a huge lack of communication."

"Big-time."

He sat there for a moment, absorbing the revelation. He felt lower than a heel. "So I guess we screwed up. Or maybe you didn't and I did. I'll be a man and admit it was my fault. I misunderstood everything. I blew it."

"It doesn't matter whose fault it was," Rachel declared. "The past is just that—passed. Time has made us very different people. You have your life and I have mine. I just don't want some history and some silly parental fantasy muddling what has to be my main focus—getting back to New York and my career."

"Yeah," Colin said, not liking that one bit. The waiter

refilled Colin's coffee cup, and as he did, Colin signaled for the check. Although he really wasn't ready to leave, they both had to work tomorrow and he knew they should be getting back. He watched Rachel as she polished off the last few bites of his flan before she reached for the white linen napkin and wiped her mouth.

Damn. He'd always been attracted to Rachel. Bruce had been right all along, and Colin had been too blind to realize what was, literally, right next door. He'd always had women hit on him, and the only one he'd wanted—well, she'd been his all along and he'd missed the signs.

Now it was too late.

THEY WERE QUIET on the flight back. He'd turned on the XM Radio, and Rachel found herself too emotionally charged to nod off on the return trip to Morrisville.

Colin had admitted prom had been a big misunderstanding. He'd liked her.

That maybe she'd been wrong all these years ago had her reevaluating everything she'd ever thought about Colin Morris. Sure, they'd both grown up. They were now different people. High school was everyone's worst nightmare and, twenty years later, their fondest memory. Time healed all wounds, and Rachel was licking new ones from Marco, ones she knew she'd eventually get over. She was strong. Determined.

As for Colin, she could understand a communication glitch. The teenage years were giant soap operas where insecurities wrote the script. Very few, if any, teens mastered being a wordsmith. The risk of rejection was too great to practice communication skills. Still…she was just a little in shock that he'd liked her back.

"We'll be landing in twenty minutes. We've just passed Indianapolis," Colin told her.

Rachel adjusted her microphone. "Okay."

"Have you been sleeping?" he asked.

"No." She waited to hear if he'd say anything else, but Colin remained silent. He didn't speak again until he announced they were changing altitude.

His voice came to her ear. "There are the runway lights."

Rachel looked out the window at the parallel lines below. Within minutes, they were on the ground and Colin had parked the plane in its spot.

"Careful now," he said as he opened her door and helped her out. Her hand trembled in his as he assisted her down. Could she ever touch him again? Somehow the only thing clearing the air had done was make her even more aware of the person Colin had become.

"I've got it this time," she said, trying to lighten the moment. "Thanks."

"Good. Here are my car keys. It's gotten a little chilly. Go ahead and start the car while I finish up."

"You're sure you don't want me to wait here?"

"I don't want you getting cold. Here. If you would, just take my bag." Colin opened the door in the tail and handed her his duffel bag. "That would be great. Thanks."

"Sure." Rachel took it and soon had it and herself stashed in the car. She was used to northeast chill, but the open spaces of Morrisville seemed colder. Maybe that old saying about concrete holding in the heat was true.

Colin joined her a few minutes later. "You should have turned on the engine," he chided, closing the driver's door behind him.

"I didn't want to waste any gas."

"I'd rather you not have been sitting here shivering," he said as he fired up the engine. "It'll be a minute or two before the car gets warm. You've got a seat heater. The switch is on your right."

Soon Rachel felt the heat coming from beneath the leather. Colin put the car in Drive and headed back toward town.

"I had a nice time," Rachel said, the silence now deafening.

"Good," Colin said. He was bothered by something, and Rachel wasn't sure what.

"Are you okay? You seem really put out."

Colin tapped his hands on the steering wheel. "No, it's nothing. Just realized I'd forgotten to do some things at home."

"Oh," she said, not certain whether he was telling her the truth. An element had changed since dinner, and whatever it was, Rachel didn't like it.

Moments later, he pulled into the driveway of Rachel's house. Their reservation had been for seven and the meal leisurely. The clock on the dashboard read a quarter to twelve. The house was dark, Rachel's grandmother and mother having retired long ago. "I guess we were out late," he said.

"I had a good time," Rachel repeated. "Thank you for dinner. It was fun getting out of Morrisville. I haven't been to Chicago since I was a kid."

"I love Chicago. It's my second city. I never felt the need to move there, since I can fly up anytime."

"Living in a city is different," Rachel said. "It took me a while to get used to it. So many people and so many things going on. But I adjusted. I found myself there, I think."

"That's from a movie," he said.

"Caught me." Rachel grinned. "*Sabrina.* She said she

found herself in Paris. I liked the one with Audrey Hepburn better. She went to Paris to attend cooking school. In the modern version, Sabrina works at *Vogue*."

"I saw both," Colin said. "She thought she was in love with one brother and fell in love with the other."

"That's right." Rachel said, impressed he'd seen both chick flicks.

"Amazing how confusion happens," Colin said. He drew a breath. "I should probably be going. I've got an 8:00 a.m. meeting tomorrow."

"I won't be heading into the diner until eleven. I'll do the lunch rush and then start baking."

"If you don't need to see it first, I'll mail you that letter I sent to Marco," he said.

"You could bring it by when it's done," Rachel offered, suddenly as confused as a high-school girl. She didn't want the night to end, which was ridiculous. Colin was her lawyer, nothing more. Okay, a friend, but nothing else.

"My paralegal automatically cc's the client whenever she mails a letter to opposing counsel," Colin said.

"That's logical," Rachel said, forcing herself to reach for the door handle.

His voice stopped her. "Rachel."

She turned back. "What?"

"Did you ever wonder?"

"Wonder what?" Despite the moon, his face was hidden in shadow.

"About what would have happened had we gone to prom."

All the time, but she wasn't about to tell him that. "You were still two years older. You would have graduated, moved on to college girls. Everyone knows most high-school relationships don't last. Any interest we might have had in each other was only because we lived next door. A proximity thing."

He thought about that for a minute. "So, professional from here on out?"

"You know how Morrisville is." She cracked the car door, and the interior lights came on.

He managed a wry grin. "Yeah, I live here, so believe me, I do. You're right. We don't need that."

With his words, the atmosphere inside the car intensified. Maybe it was just the warm air from the seat heater. "We'll just put it behind us, okay?" she said.

"That would be best," Colin said. "First thing tomorrow, though, all right?" He glanced at the clock. "In ten minutes you'll be inside. Promise."

She closed the door again. "I won't lose my slipper and your car won't turn into a pumpkin?"

"No, but I have to know. Just do this for me, okay?"

"Do what?" Rachel asked. She faced him fully, and immediately knew what he meant as he moved forward and his lips found hers.

"Just one kiss," he whispered. "I want the answer."

She had no idea what the question was, but the moment his lips touched, any protest fled. Colin had been her playmate, her crush. In her heart, she understood the answer he was seeking. She sought it, too, and to find it, she kissed him back.

She should feel nothing. Oh, some pleasure, yes, but not the intensity traveling through her body and scaring the life out of her. Her feelings for him had never died. Even after leaving adolescence, she still wanted him, only now with a grown-up body that craved to mate with his. She desired all she'd been denied.

But instinct wouldn't dictate her life anymore. She made her own choices. She was not staying in Morrisville and marrying Colin Morris and having his babies—although the making-love-to-him part sounded divine. His touch would erase Marco's and take her places never imagined, just as it was doing now.

She pulled away, breathless from his kiss. "Question answered?"

"Yeah," Colin said, his voice husky. Rachel attempted to tune out his sexy tone. The clock flickered to 11:59.

"I've got to go. You have an early meeting."

"Don't worry, professional from here on out. Just friends," Colin said. "This kiss— Thank you. It…"

"Laid some ghosts to rest?"

"Yeah, okay." If he had something different to say, he chose to keep it to himself.

"Well, for me, too," Rachel lied. All his kiss had done was make her long for more. She pulled on the handle and pushed the door open. Cold air flooded the inside of the car, making her shiver. "Thanks for tonight. I'll see you soon."

With that, she shut the door behind her and hurried into the house. Less than eight minutes later, she was curled up under the flannel sheets and turning on the electric blanket.

She put a finger to her lips, noticing their swollen tenderness. Colin had kissed her. Closure. A final kiss to put the past and their silly school crushes behind them. From here on out, they would be nothing more than businesslike.

A tiny sense of melancholy settled over her as she closed her eyes. Somehow, after a kiss that had rocked her world, the aftermath seemed a waste.

COLIN DROVE HOME, mindful to keep his speed at the posted limit. After kissing Rachel, he wanted nothing more than to floor the gas pedal and drive all-out.

He'd wanted to kiss her and prove to himself that nothing passionate existed. That it would be like kissing a sister. Chaste. Platonic.

He'd been wrong.

Kissing Rachel had been hot and heavy. To use one of her quotations: like the earth moved. He hadn't had sex in a car since college, but he'd have had no problem taking Rachel right then and there. Darn, he was going to be lousy for his meeting, and not from lack of sleep.

The whole situation could be summed up in one word—*frustrating*. She wanted New York; he wouldn't leave Morrisville. Nothing between them could work.

He wasn't the kind of guy to settle for less than everything, and he'd always wanted that everything with Rachel. He'd envied Bruce for years, thinking how lucky his best friend would be when he woke up and realized Rachel was his dream woman.

Well, Colin had gotten that completely wrong. Christina was Bruce's other half.

Which left Rachel…

In New York.

Chapter Six

"I can't believe you kissed Colin Morris again."

Rachel furtively glanced around her friend Heather's kitchen. Busy changing a diaper while watching a basketball game on TV in the adjoining family room, Heather's husband, Keith, wasn't paying the least bit of attention to the two women, who were just on the other side of the half wall dividing the rooms.

"I never should have told you," Rachel said, holding her red-wine glass aloft as Heather wiped down the kitchen table in front of Rachel.

"Of course you should have," Heather said, expertly arcing the dishcloth and landing it in the sink. "I was there from the beginning, remember? Who else had listened to your mooning over the man since eighth grade?"

"Yeah, you have," Rachel said, nostalgia sweeping through her. The same age, she and Heather had been pals ever since the third grade when Heather's family had relocated from Saint Louis.

Rachel had even been one of Heather's bridesmaids three years ago, standing next to Heather's sister, who had served as matron of honor. Rachel had made a weekend jaunt home for the wedding, but she hadn't contacted Bruce or Colin. Maybe she should have. Colin had been offended that she'd simply "ditched him." Of course, that was what she'd been trying to do all these years.

Finished diapering, Keith held his ten-month-old daughter aloft. The basketball game was on halftime break and the TV showed a bunch of announcers conversing. "It's Erin's bedtime. I'll put her down so you two can catch up," Keith announced.

"Mama wants a kiss," Heather told her daughter, and after giving her child a peck on the cheek, Keith made an airplane noise and flew baby Erin away.

Now that Keith was out of earshot, Heather sat down and reached for the bottle of red wine Rachel had brought. "You sure haven't had a lot of this," she said as she topped off both glasses.

"I'm good," Rachel said as Heather returned the bottle to the center of the table. "Keith seems like a great dad. You've found a gem."

"I have. He's the best husband and he's wonderful with Erin," Heather said, lifting her glass. She thought a moment. "Let's toast. Cheers."

Rachel raised her wineglass and tilted her head. "Yes, but to what?"

Heather shrugged. "To your visit. To your presence being more than just a fast in and out. To getting rid of some stuck-on-himself fiancé who probably wouldn't have let me be in his wedding. I'll drink to all that."

"Me, too," Rachel agreed as they clinked glasses. "And unfortunately, you're correct. Marco pretty much insisted that the bridal party be from his side of the family. Looking back, I should have clued in then."

Rachel shifted and reclined farther back in the chair. "For a guy so focused on tradition, he had no problem with usurping my responsibilities and decisions. I stupidly insisted I pay for some things. Now I wish I hadn't. My foolish pride cost me a fortune I didn't have, and for naught."

"When you would call me and tell me about him, I knew he wasn't right for you," Heather announced between sips of wine. "But you seemed happy, and who was I to ruin that? No one likes to rain on anyone's parade."

"Hindsight's twenty-twenty and I wish you had. Although I can understand why you didn't. At the time I was too blinded to believe Marco was anything but romance-novel perfect. I guess I don't have very good judgment in men, especially if I let Colin kiss me!"

"You cannot fault yourself for that. Chalk the experience up to curiosity. You know, like seeing if his lips made your toes curl when you were sober. In high school you'd both had champagne. So did they?"

Rachel chewed on her lower lip. His kiss had made her ready to throw caution to the wind and lose herself in more ways than just kissing. She nodded.

Heather's body twitched and she shook herself. "Sorry. Being gross and picturing. Lucky you. Not that Keith doesn't make me scream…well, you get the picture. No need to provide too much information. But girlfriend, a kiss like that is rare. I wasn't as pristine and picky as you. I imbibed a little during college. Some of the sex I had was simply sloppy and not worth the energy. But when I met Keith, then I learned what making love meant. There's never a time I don't feel the entire connection—mental, physical and spiritual."

"It was a kiss. One to put the past behind us. Surely

that's all it was. And no way am I planning on making love with Colin. What am I to do—abandon myself to a torrid affair until I leave? My life is in New York. Can you see me here in Morrisville, playing house?"

"I play house every day. I wouldn't have it any other way," Heather said flatly.

Rachel frowned. Trust her to have sounded insensitive. "I'm sorry. I didn't mean to imply that…" Rachel apologized. She certainly didn't mean to suggest that Heather had settled when she'd married the blue-collar line worker she'd met at the factory in Batesville. Heather had completed her MBA work online and had been on the fast corporate track when she'd fallen hard for Keith. With the arrival of Erin, she'd taken a leave of absence to stay home, walking away from a five-figure salary. She and Keith lived in a modest ranch house that they afforded using only his income.

"I know you didn't mean to sound bratty, so I'll forgive you this time," Heather said with a grin. "I've known you far too long to be insulted that easily. Besides, you know where all my skeletons are hidden."

Rachel smiled. "That I do. Although I won't tell." Warm-and-fuzzy sentiment had her adding, "You are the best."

"I know," Heather said flippantly, sipping more wine. "Seriously, though. You're just different. I'm content with my simple life. I don't need fancy jewels and stuff like that. I'm happy staying home. I find it fulfilling. But not you. You've always wanted that pie in the sky. You've always been grasping for something."

"Ha on the pie-in-the-sky quip. But you've got the rest correct. I have these ambitions and I can't deny myself trying to achieve them. You fit here. You'll take Erin to the park this summer. Hang out at the country-club pool. That type of life would drive me insane. I don't know how my mother and grandmother do it, tolerating people like Elmer and Harold on a daily basis. I don't belong here."

"Without the right man, you don't. You'd be screaming in frustration within the first two weeks if you had to live here as a single woman. Not that I don't think you'll make a good mom or anything. Don't you dare go out and tell people I said that."

"I just might," Rachel teased. She toyed absently with her wineglass, making the wine inside form a little current. "Marco wanted at least four kids. He wanted me barefoot and pregnant in the kitchen. The prospect scared the crud out of me."

"That's because he wasn't right for you. When you find your match, everything clicks. You want to be with him and bear his children. It's the most natural feeling in the world and it's not describable. You can't search for it. You just know when you've found that nirvana."

Heather sipped her wine and then stared at the glass. "This is really great stuff. You're going to get me tipsy. I only stopped breast-feeding two months ago. This is a treat. I haven't imbibed in ages."

"Thanks." Rachel didn't tell her that she'd brought the vintage with her from New York, or that it retailed for seventy dollars a bottle. "I bought the bottle to go with this steak dish I'd planned to cook for Marco. Seemed like tonight was a good night to drink the thing without him, plus you cooked a great meal."

"His loss," Heather said, grabbing the bottle. "Want any more?"

"I'm fine," Rachel answered, covering the rim of the wineglass with the palm of her hand.

"Good." Heather poured the remnants into her own glass. "Beware, honey," she called to Keith, who was entering the kitchen. "I'm getting tipsy. You know what that means."

"Yep." Keith gave Heather a secret smile as he passed by and returned to the family room.

"I think you should let yourself go," Heather told Rachel suddenly.

"Huh?" Not quite following the shift in their conversation, Rachel stared at her friend. Heather was nodding as if she'd just had the best idea in years.

"Yeah. With Colin. Sample the man. I think that after all this time, he'd be the perfect rebound guy for you to lose yourself in for a while. Like you said, you're going back to New York. You already have the perfect escape clause. Moving is the great way to end things."

Maybe every last drop of wine had traveled to Heather's head. A bottle held a little more than four glasses and she'd easily had more than two. Keith, not into wine, had had a small portion and then switched to iced tea with dinner.

"It's been, what—almost two weeks since you've seen him?" Heather asked.

"Yeah. He hasn't even come into the diner to eat. It's almost as if he's avoiding me. His dad's there just about every day. Not that I should have noticed. Since word got out that I'm baking for hire, I'm swamped. This is a wacky year with St. Patrick's Day this upcoming Monday and Palm Sunday the very day before. To get ready this week I've been cooking something every day. Not only have I had the stuff for the diner, but I've had tons of cake orders, and before Saturday night I have to make six hundred shamrock cookies for the Knights of Columbus annual corned-beef-and-cabbage shindig."

"That's two days from now. We'll be there, won't we, Keith?"

They got a grunt from Keith, who'd settled into a La-Z-Boy recliner. "We always go," Heather said. "Dinner, dancing and green beer. This year I can have a glass. Got to love it."

Used to the huge celebrations and the supersize parade through Manhattan, Rachel simply nodded her agreement. "Sounds like a lot of fun."

"You should come with us. You'll recognize most of the people who'll be there. It's a diverse crowd. Lots of people our age. Most of the town shows up, as does everyone else from the surrounding areas."

Rachel shook her head, rejecting the offer. "Thanks, but no. I will have finally finished all those cookies and I'll be exhausted. Besides, I'm not ready to be out on the Morrisville social scene."

"Not even to find a rebound guy?"

"Not even."

"Too bad. Lance Gordon just got divorced. He's a great catch. His wife was a gold digger. Luckily, there were no kids. She didn't get anything, and she moved back to Terre Haute."

"Not interested." Lance was another schoolmate in their graduating class. His family owned several gas stations.

"So I guess it's just Colin you're pining for. I mean, why else would he kiss you?"

"Maybe he did it to see if *his* toes curled." Rachel exhaled her frustration at the question that had been consuming her for two weeks. "I don't know. I've never been able to figure out the man, and I grew up next door to him and sent him messages using Morse code. He said he liked me during high school. I don't get it. If the kiss was important, wouldn't he come around to see me? All I got was the copy of the letter he sent to Marco."

Heather winced. "Ouch."

"Exactly. It's like he thinks this kiss was a big mistake. It's lousy déjà vu all over again."

"Hang in there," Heather consoled her.

"Trying." Rachel finished the wine in her glass. At least she'd shared the bottle with friends.

"You've heard nothing from Marco's camp yet?" Heather asked.

Rachel sighed and set her wineglass aside. "No. I'm not sure if no news is good news. I'm hoping so, though. I could use some good fortune to come my way."

"It will," Heather said with a vigorous nod. She grimaced. "Ouch. I don't usually drink wine. I really haven't had anything to drink since nine months before Erin. Wait—did I already say that? Hangovers and early-rising babies don't mix."

"Think of tonight as preparation for the green beer you'll have this Saturday."

"Clearly I need practice. I've turned into a lightweight if this is all it took to get me tipsy. Luckily the Knights of Columbus is only two blocks over. Unless it's really cold, we'll walk. That way neither of us has to worry about being a designated driver or where the car keys are. Keith's mom is babysitting. He and I haven't had a night to ourselves in forever. Not that I've minded," Heather added hastily. "But I can't wait just to have a totally uninterrupted night. You really should meet us there. It'll be fun."

"I'll think about it," Rachel conceded, wondering when she'd last "let go." Since her relocation to New York, she couldn't remember one time that she'd behaved as if she didn't have a care in the world.

She knew Heather and Keith wouldn't really tie one on at the Knights of Columbus hall and get totally drunk, yet the idea of being able to simply have fun without worrying about appearances was appealing. Heck, in Morrisville you still didn't have to lock your doors, meaning that Heather and Keith could spend St. Patrick's Day with only one focus—each other.

"Speaking of going, I should probably be leaving," Rachel said. The clock on Heather's oven had just flipped to 9:00 p.m.

"So soon?" Heather asked.

"I've got to get up early tomorrow. My grandma has to meet a vendor, so I told her I'd be at the diner at eight. I'll be doing a twelve-hour day. My Friday-night fun will be cooking at Kim's."

"If you want, I can always help you take cookies. My mother-in-law would be more than happy to babysit Erin two nights in a row. She's already spoiled my daughter silly. It can't get worse and Erin loves her."

"I may take you up on that, but for now, go attack your husband and make him a happy man," Rachel said, rising to her feet.

"I always do," Heather said, standing, as well.

"Gosh, it's been great seeing you," Rachel said suddenly, awed by the intensity of her feelings. She'd missed Heather. Rachel had had a few friends in New York, but she'd never been this close to any of them. "I don't have anyone like you in New York."

"That's because I'm so original, which is just one more reason for you not to be such a stranger," Heather said, embarrassed, yet pleased. "And I definitely expect to hear more about a certain guy, especially if the situation calls for it."

"Ha," Rachel said. "Our kiss was probably just an aberration, something not to be repeated in this lifetime."

"Yeah, right. Keep lying to yourself, because I don't believe it. Keith, Rachel's leaving," Heather called.

Keith got up and ambled over. He gave Rachel a quick hug, then returned to watch the final moments of the basketball game.

"Let me walk you to the door," Heather said. She led the way to the tiny foyer. "I'm serious about you not being a stranger. Let's see each other more often now that you're back, get into those mundane activities you claim to despise so much. You remember Kristin, Colin's sister? Well, she's having one of those jewelry parties Tuesday night. Let me know if you want to go."

The offer was both sweet and petrifying. Home parties were things married women did, right? Shopping for jewelry was to be done at places like Tiffany or Cartier or one of those exclusive designer shops. Then again, Rachel had left that lifestyle behind. Maybe she should try to fit in here. Doing so would allow her to spend more time with Heather. "If I'm not swamped baking Easter cakes, I'll try to make it. I'll call you," Rachel said, giving Heather a hug.

Friday and Saturday were both busy, and Rachel exhaled a sigh of relief as she shut down the oven Sunday evening. With Palm Sunday and St. Patrick's Day on top of each other, she'd taken on way too many orders. But she'd accepted them all, knowing that after Easter the frantic pace would end. April would be pretty slow, maybe just the occasional birthday or anniversary cake. At this moment, getting as much cash as possible into her pocket was the priority.

Rachel finished her cleanup and finally locked the doors more than fourteen hours after she'd first started working. Kim's Diner never closed except on Christmas and Easter, but her mother had taken the entire day off to attend Palm Sunday services and visit with her sister, Rachel's aunt, in nearby Columbus. Rachel had clocked in at 8:00 a.m.

As if not wanting to move, Rachel's little compact coughed as she turned the ignition and pressed the gas pedal. As always, no lights were on in the family home when she arrived. Her grandmother and mother had already retired for the night. They'd be up early, getting ready for the St. Patrick's Day feast. The diner had smelled of corned beef all day in preparation.

Rachel parked her car off to the side so she wouldn't be blocking anyone tomorrow morning. She removed her keys from the ignition, opened the driver's door and stepped out—

And froze when a big bulky figure pounded through an opening in the bushes.

"Rachel! Thank God it's finally you. I've been waiting forever for you to get home! I need your help."

Chapter Seven

Colin's surprise arrival had her quaking in her tennis shoes. She attempted to calm her rapid heartbeat, chiding herself that she was in Morrisville, safest place on the planet, and not New York, where any stranger could be dangerous and you always had to be on your guard.

She took a deep breath. What in the world did Colin require at this late hour? "You need my help?"

"Yes. I need cupcakes. I told Libby—she's my niece. Have you met Libby?"

"The twins."

He nodded. "Yes. I said that I'd bring the cupcakes for her school's St. Patrick's Day luncheon tomorrow. She's responsible for a class set and her mother—my sister Kristin—has had her hands full this weekend. She hosted her husband's family for dinner tonight. So I volunteered for the job."

"Okay. You've lost me. You couldn't just drive into Greensburg for some cupcakes? Wal-Mart's open twenty-four hours. They always have a great selection. Probably have plenty with plastic shamrock rings for garnish. Kids Libby's age love those."

Colin winced. "I found out a few hours ago that Libby sort of bragged to her classmates that she's bringing your cupcakes. Kristin called me as soon as she learned about it. I told her I hadn't gotten anything and that I'd ask you. I don't think children realize what 'last minute' means. Kristin was extremely apologetic, if that helps. She's speaking to Libby about this, but still, I'm Libby's guest of honor at her school lunch tomorrow."

Rachel sighed. "And you couldn't have called me earlier? You've been waiting at your parents' house, stalking me?"

"Guilty. I drove by the diner, but I was more worried you'd panic if I banged on the door. And I've been trying all night to phone you. I left you three voice mails on your cell and the diner phone is on automatic answering machine after three."

"We set that to a standard message. It doesn't even ring."

"I know how much this puts you out. Really I do. You'll earn my and Kristin's undying gratitude. I mean, I guess I could go to Wal-Mart and pass their cupcakes off as yours."

"Absolutely not." Rachel dug into her purse, noting that her phone had shut itself off, which meant any calls would automatically route to voice mail. She grimaced. "My battery is probably dead. I forgot to charge my phone last night."

He appeared so earnest, standing there in jeans and crew sweater.

"My mom said you could use her kitchen, if that helps any."

Rachel shook her head. "All my St. Patrick's Day stuff is at the diner. It took me forever, but I finished the Knights of Columbus cookies yesterday with an hour to spare."

"They were really good, too," Colin complimented her.

"The hit of the party. Everyone raved about how delicious they were."

Rachel doubted that but warmed to his flattery. "Wait. You were there?"

"I dropped by for a little while. An hour or so earlier in the evening. Saw your friend Heather and her husband, Keith. She said you had dinner with them Thursday night and that you were probably home resting from your cookiefest."

Could Morrisville get any smaller? Rachel turned her phone on, noting she had five voice mails and an empty battery. One message had to be from Heather, calling about running into Colin. "I was. Baking and frosting those consumed a lot more time than I expected. Get in," she told him.

Even after his earnest declaration, he still seemed surprised by her action. "You'll help me?"

"What type of friend would I be if I didn't? And I'm certainly not going to break some little girl's heart or let you pass off some other company's baked goods as mine. As if."

She opened the driver's door to her sedan and Colin climbed into the other side. Unlike his newer car, hers was eight years old and showed some real wear and tear. He didn't appear to notice. "I owe you one."

"Take it off my bill," she quipped.

"Speaking of your legal matters, I got a reply from Marco's attorney. It's nothing, just a standard acknowledgment that they received my letter and will be getting back to me after consulting with their client. The dance has started."

"I'll be glad when the dance is over," Rachel replied, driving the short distance back to the diner. She pulled into the parking spot, unlocked the diner door and deactivated the alarm she'd programmed less than twenty minutes ago. Because Morrisville was so safe, her grandmother hadn't really seen the need for a burglar alarm, but the system had come paired with the monitored smoke alarms Kim had installed during the rebuild after the fire.

Rachel flipped a switch and light flooded the kitchen. "Since some kids are allergic to chocolate, the quickest thing will be for me to whip together a yellow cake batter and frost the cupcakes with a buttercream icing that I'll color green and top with green and white sprinkles. They won't be anything fancy, but they'll be from Sweet Sensations."

"Sweet Sensations?"

She shrugged out of her coat and hung it on a hook. "I've decided that's the name of my baking company. I'm still in the planning stages, but I figured a name would probably be step one."

"Sweet Sensations. I like it," Colin said. "When you get ready for step two, let me know. I've helped quite a few start-ups write their business plans."

"I'm already overwhelmed trying to figure everything out. I have no idea how to run, much less start, a business. I've been watching my grandmother all week and still don't know how she manages everything—payroll, budget and the like. My mom's been working with me on ordering so that I always have just the right quantities on hand. Waste costs money. I did learn some of this in New York, but my job was mostly food preparation. Someone else handled the stocking details. I still have a lot to learn. I'm lucky to be able to cut my teeth here before I head back into the cutthroat world of New York City."

Rachel removed the smock hanging on a peg. She put the red broadcloth on and then found a plain white apron for Colin. "Get dressed."

He stared at the garment for a moment and then obliged. "I guess even Wolfgang Puck wears one of these."

"Yep, and he's famous," Rachel said. She reached for a wooden recipe holder and removed a card protected in a plastic sleeve. "How many cupcakes do we need?"

Colin shrugged. "I honestly have no idea. Enough for everyone in the class."

Rachel's decision was instantaneous. "We'll make thirty. Most elementary classes aren't that large—at least, I hope not. There were only about twenty people in mine."

She set the recipe in a slanted holder. "We won't have time to let the butter soften naturally, so I'm going to cheat and use the microwave."

"I doubt anyone will notice," Colin said. "They'd be happy with a box mix."

She shot Colin a disgusted look as she took a moment to wash her hands. "Yes, but *I'll* know. I refuse to have anything I bake taste plain or ordinary. A sweet should melt in your mouth, give you a rush of decadent flavor, or it's simply not worth eating. I make every calorie worth it. Can you separate eggs?"

He stared at her blankly and gave her a sheepish smile.

"Didn't think so," Rachel said with a little chuckle, her tiredness ebbing as the adrenaline of a work deadline began to flow.

"Hey, it's not my fault," Colin protested. "My mother won't let anyone in her coveted space. You must be special if she offered to let you use it tonight."

"Kitchens are sanctums. You can sift the flour," Rachel

pulled out a large stainless-steel container, measured an amount into a glass bowl and then set another same-size bowl beside it. "Wash your hands first at that sink over there. Then sift the flour in that bowl into this one." Rachel moved quickly as she put a sifter next to Colin. She added some of the flour. "Once you've poured it into the sifter, like this, then you hold it over this bowl and squeeze this handle, and the sifted flour falls in."

"Gotcha. I can do that." Colin went to wash his hands.

"Good. I didn't think you were hopeless." Rachel began to gather the other ingredients.

"I'm not. Okay, maybe a little. So you really have to sift flour? Even if it says presifted on the bag? That's the kind I buy. I keep it in the refrigerator."

"Which is smart. It'll last longer, especially if you don't use it often." She had everything out on the counter and gestured to the recipe. "Sifting makes a difference in fancier baked goods," she said, "when you're really concerned with texture and density. These cupcakes will have a texture like white cake."

"Cakes have textures?" he asked, surprised.

She smiled. "Absolutely."

"No clue what you mean, but here goes," Colin said, and began sifting the flour. Rachel felt his gaze on her as she stuck some butter in the microwave and set the program to thirty seconds at half power. When the butter was softened, she took the dish out and placed it on the stainless-steel countertop. Next she used one hand to crack six eggs, then expertly separated the whites from the yolks.

"I've never seen you at work," Colin remarked.

"Few have," she said, her hands moving like lightning as she used a wire whisk to combine the egg yolks, a cup of milk and some vanilla. She set that aside and mixed together in a large bowl the flour he'd sifted, some sugar, baking powder and salt. Next she added the melted butter and put the bowl in the mixer.

"This aerates the batter and develops the cake's structure," she told him as the mixer beat the ingredients. "Now I'll add the egg mixture."

The entire process took less than ten minutes, and soon Rachel was spooning the batter into cupcake pans. The oven behind her beeped, indicating the temperature had reached 350 degrees Fahrenheit.

"I never knew baking could be so involved," Colin commented. "I'm impressed. So, do we have a break while everything bakes?"

She shook her head. "Hardly. We have to make the crème anglaise and the Italian meringue for the buttercream icing I'm going to frost with. Stand back and let the master work. Oh, do me a favor. See that metal bowl there? Fill it halfway with ice cubes from the freezer. Thanks."

AS RACHEL CONTINUED to work, Colin simply did as he was told. His cooking consisted of microwaving, reheating and opening cans. His mother had trained the girls, but she'd been sexist in keeping the boys out of her...sanctum, as Rachel had called the kitchen.

So Colin, never one to turn down a learning opportunity, observed Rachel work, her movements fluid and graceful. Whatever crème anglaise was, it involved cooking milk and vanilla in one pan, then adding this to a sugar-and-egg-yolk mixture cooking in another pan.

Rachel stirred constantly, measuring the concoction's temperature with a thin silver thermometer. Once heated, she strained the mixture into a small bowl, which she placed inside the bowl filled with ice. "This will help the crème anglaise cool faster while I make the meringue."

Soon Rachel was also setting the stiffened egg whites off to one side.

"Now, before the cupcakes come out and while this stuff cools, I'll beat this butter." Rachel used the microwave to soften a few more sticks. "After that, all that's left is to add the crème anglaise and meringue to the butter and we have our frosting."

"Ah." He stood there, his arms at his sides. Guilt plagued him. "I really didn't mean to have you do this much work."

"It's nothing," she said. "I do this routinely. I love it. I'm tired from being on my feet all day, but I'm pretending tonight is practice for one of those cooking competitions where they give you a certain time limit to create your masterpiece."

He winced and stepped toward her. "It wasn't my intention to put you under any pressure. I thought you came in late today—not that that's an excuse or rationalization."

"My mom went to church this morning. I didn't help open since Gail filled in. I got here at eight. Hey, I have a few of those cookies left from last night. Rejects that didn't make the quality cut. Want one?"

Rachel went over to a small storage container and pulled off the lid. She tilted the plastic, revealing five cookies. "I promise you they're still good. I just messed up on the frosting on this one. See?"

Colin couldn't tell what was wrong with the cookie. Was she talking about the little wiggle in the middle of the straight line of piped icing? He could hardly tell the cookie wasn't perfect. He grabbed a shamrock and bit off the stem. "Delicious."

She smiled and wiped her hands on her apron. "Thanks. I usually don't eat what I bake, but I need a little sugar in my bloodstream." Rachel bit into her own cookie and momentarily closed her eyes as she savored the flavor. "I always liked this recipe."

Colin's mouth dried as he watched Rachel swallow. He set his cookie on the counter. "Mind if I grab a cola?"

"Help yourself. Bring me one, too, will you?" Rachel took another bite and Colin escaped by going out into the main restaurant area. She had no idea what a temptress she was. He was finding impartiality hard to maintain, especially after their kiss. He brought back two full glasses. "Here you go."

"Thanks. Want the last cookie?" She dangled the container.

"I'm fine," he said. What he'd like was to kiss her again. "I still have this one to finish."

Rachel replaced the lid. "I certainly don't need the calories. Three is already over my limit. I can't believe I scarfed them down."

"They're that good. I already told you everyone last night loved them." To control his libido, he took another bite.

She leaned her hip against the counter. "They did turn out okay. I'm glad. Cookies are one of my favorite things. They're time-consuming, though. I did every one of them by hand."

"You shouldn't tire yourself out," Colin said, suddenly concerned.

She shook her head and he had an urge to remove her ball cap and run his hands through her hair. "I don't mind. Cooking is manual labor. Like a massage therapist's hands, mine are well trained."

Colin finished his cookie and drank a large gulp of soda.

Did she not know the impact of her words? He opened and closed his mouth.

"What? You were about to say something but stopped," Rachel said, edging closer.

"I was imagining those hands on me," he admitted. He grimaced as he realized he'd answered her aloud. She was now staring at him, her brown eyes wide.

"Sorry. You mentioned your hands, then massage. Just forget it. I'm a male. You know how testosterone works. My mind went somewhere unprofessional and it shouldn't have. Won't happen again."

Could he not do anything right tonight? Already he'd coerced her into baking, and now he sounded like a pathetic sex maniac. He feared she'd think the worst.

"You've just been too long without dating someone," Rachel said as the kitchen timer beeped, indicating the cupcake pans needed to be turned so the cupcakes would brown evenly.

Yep, she'd misconstrued his words. He certainly wasn't communicating correctly. The next few seconds didn't help. She took out a steel tester, opened the lower oven and bent over to check the batter.

"Don't do that again," he said, his tone huskier than usual. The view had been way too enticing.

Rachel's brow creased and she frowned at him. "Do what?"

"Bend over. Whatever you do, don't do that."

HE'D BEEN LOOKING at her backside. Of all the... She bristled. She and Colin had said they would be professional. Why was he staring at her like that? Good grief. Rachel's patience was wearing thin. She was doing him a favor and he was ogling her. Part of her liked the attention, but the other, more rational, side of her acknowledged his attention for what it was.

Lust.

She put the tester on the counter. "Well, I used the lower oven, so I have to bend over. Just stop looking. You're a man. You know how to turn around. Perhaps you need to go out on the prowl. Date some woman. Eject some hormones. This has to be a dry spell or something for you," she said.

"I am not a playboy and that's hardly my problem," Colin said with a knifelike edge in his voice that had her assessing him again. "Not in the slightest. I like sex as much as the next guy, but it's not something I can't live without. It's not like substituting chocolate for vanilla."

"Actually, you wouldn't substitute those ingredients…"

His blue-eyed gaze intensified. "Poor analogy. It doesn't matter. The fact is, you've never given yourself enough credit where I'm concerned, have you?"

Surely he couldn't mean… "What do you mean by that?"

Colin closed the gap between them, invading her space. She could smell his aftershave, sense the tension he kept checked. "I don't think you realize the power you have over me. You are pure torture, Rachel Palladia. You're right under my nose and perfectly untouchable. I'm not sure how much more of this I can stand. I've tried to avoid you for two weeks. If I hadn't needed cupcakes…" He trailed off. "We've shared two kisses and they aren't enough."

"You can't be serious. My words were to clear up the past, not make the present worse—for anyone." She tried to make light of the situation. "You're being silly. Thinking too much. Being too deep. We're different people now.

You kissed me. I kissed you back. We felt some heat. Chemistry. We're adults. Chalk the kiss up to curiosity."

"Which still means, as you said that night, we ought to know better," Colin said.

"I believe that's what I said," Rachel replied. She turned to put the used mixing bowls in the sink. "You and I getting involved in any way beyond friendship would be…"

One of the stainless-steel bowls slipped out of her hand and dropped into the sink with a clatter. Her mouth couldn't form the word *mistake*. If they got involved, it would be fabulous. She'd be able to touch his skin, feel him pressed to her. His lips…oh, those on her lips would be divine. Like one of her sweets. Worth every calorie.

But that was the trouble with desserts. Too many made you gain weight. The momentary bliss wore off, to be replaced with long-term effects. "Well…friends. That's enough. Neither of us needs any more complication than we already have in our lives. Right?"

"I don't know," Colin said. "For the first time, I'm pretty confused. Here. Let me help you."

"I'll get it." He'd come even closer, carrying a bowl in front of him like an offering. "You could take the cupcakes out," Rachel said, relieved when the oven timer beeped. Fate had intervened—for once with perfect timing—to get her out of what was fast becoming a sticky situation. "Just put on those pot holders, remove the pans carefully and place them on the racks I set out. Don't turn the pans over."

"Okay." He handed her the bowl, their fingers brushing as he deposited it in her hands. Then he was the one bending over, removing the pans and setting them out to cool. Her throat constricted and she turned away, talking to him while not looking at him.

"We'll have to let the cupcakes remain in the pans ten minutes before we take them out." She reached over and set the timer. "The cupcakes have to be totally cool before I can frost them, so I'm thinking I'll finish cleaning up now and come in first thing in the morning to ice them. I could have them all done by 10:00 a.m. You want them by lunch, right?"

She glanced at him. He'd removed the oven mitts. "I'm supposed to be at Libby's school at eleven."

"Then that's what we'll do," she said, settling the matter. "I'll leave a note for my grandma to let her know what's going on."

"Okay," Colin said. "I'll be in around ten-thirty to pick them up."

"That would be fine." She made her tone brisk...professional, but he'd returned to stand less than a foot away from her. He reached out and brushed her cheekbone. "You had something on your face."

"Oh." His mere touch had her body reacting, a little tingle that had sent an involuntary twitch through her shoulders. "Probably icing. You should have seen me at the end of making those cookies. I had green frosting everywhere."

His eyes darkened and she realized her mistake. "I would have liked that," he told her.

He reached for a beater she hadn't yet put in the sink. He ran his fingertip along it, scooping off the buttercream frosting left there. Then put his finger in his mouth. "Good stuff."

"Glad you like it," she said, far too aware of his proximity. She'd already placed the bowl of frosting in the refrigerator. "I'll add green food coloring tomorrow and..."

Her voice trailed off as Colin scraped the beater again, capturing more frosting. He pressed the frosting against her partially open lips. She automatically sucked his finger, tasting the morsel he'd offered her. "It *is* good," she said, swallowing, trying to regain her composure.

"I'd like to see you covered with icing," Colin said, his voice low and deep as he removed the last of the frosting from the beater, then decreased the gap between them to mere inches. "I could think of a lot of creative ways to clean it off you."

"Mmm-hmm," Rachel mumbled, determined not to open her mouth.

She should stop him. Say no. Do something.

But she stood there, letting Colin spread frosting over her top lip, then her lower lip. She watched him, transfixed. Even with all the time she'd spent in Marco's kitchen, he'd never done anything this erotic.

He'd never touched her like this, making her quiver with anticipation.

Sex had been basic. Ordinary. Bland. Rote. Boring.

Nothing like the high intensity surrounding this very moment.

Time seemed to stretch as every one of her senses heightened, she waited to see what Colin would do next, even though she knew—he was going to kiss her. And no matter how resolved she was to just be friends, she was going to kiss him back. She couldn't resist him. Didn't want to. Never had. Wasn't sure why she was pretending otherwise.

He lowered his mouth to hers, and with the lightest of touches his tongue came forward and gently licked the frosting from her lips. Then somehow her hands were in his hair and she lost herself, let herself revel in the pleasure his touch provided.

His kisses tasted of sweet frosting and something more

she couldn't classify. And then she stopped trying to figure everything out but simply gave herself to the moment. He'd pulled her toward him, cupping her bottom and pressing her body to his, his movement letting her feel exactly what she was doing to him and how much he wanted her.

She could kiss him forever, she thought hazily. She wouldn't stop with kissing, either. She wanted the whole thing— At that moment, the timer she'd set when he'd taken out the cupcakes from the oven started buzzing.

"I guess the cupcakes are ready to be stored," Colin said, pulling away.

"They can wait a minute," she said, not wanting the moment to end.

"Don't want to dry them out." He stepped away from her, severing the connection.

"Uh, no. We don't," Rachel replied, trying to regroup. She removed all the cupcakes from the pans and properly stored them so that they would cool some more but not dry out. Then she loaded a few last dishes. "We're done here," she said flatly.

He shook his head. "No. Let's get something straight for once. We're done baking. You—me? We're not done. Not by a long shot."

His words thrilled her. Wasn't this what she'd desired? Colin Morris wanting her? Still… "Look, we can't keep kissing each other."

He waited, his posture daring her to continue.

"I'm not saying I didn't enjoy it. I did," she admitted, flustered that she couldn't find the perfect words for what she wanted to say. "But you and I can't get involved."

"We already are," Colin stated. "Trying to stop this…

us…is like trying to save the *Titanic* from sinking. A failing proposition. Impossible. I've spent two weeks trying."

"We're only going to hurt each other," Rachel protested. "We both know I'm leaving. I'd hate to return in three years, meet your wife and feel all awkward and weird. Our families are friends. You know we'll run into each other. It's inevitable. This is so hard. I'm torn. I admit, I'd love to get together with you. It's like my childhood fantasy come to life."

He stood there, mulling over what she'd said. Impatient, she added, "But we're geographically challenged. I'm not going to get hot and heavy with you every time I visit. I'm not going to be a weekend girl. You might have a plane, but flying up to New York to see me every so often is silly. We're doomed to failure, and neither of us wants that. Believe me, I've thought about it."

He shifted his weight. "About 'it'?"

She clarified. "You."

"Me."

"Geez. Do I have to spell it out? Making love with you. I've thought about it. Dreamed of it, actually." She wrung her hands in frustration. "I don't believe we're having this conversation. This whole night has gotten surreal. It's like being on a bad sitcom where the writers have all disappeared."

"It's probably a good thing we are talking," Colin told her. "We failed to talk in high school after our first kiss and look where that got us. A big load of misunderstanding and BS that we both carried like bad baggage into every subsequent relationship."

"Now who's giving himself more credit?" she quipped.

"You know I'm right."

Rachel could tell he wasn't amused at her attempt to make light of the situation. "Okay, so you are. I was deeply hurt. You were my ideal."

He shifted his weight, took a step forward and then stopped. "And what if I still am? What if you are mine? We might have let all this time go by, but what if this is our second chance? Do we let this chance slide by or do we grasp the brass ring, take our bonus ride and risk the chance the ride might not stop?"

"It has to stop. Nothing good lasts," she said stubbornly. He was making way too much sense, and his rationality frightened her. He was Morrisville. She was New York. She clung to that.

"You're wrong," he told her. "Your parents? Grandparents? My parents? I'm sure they'd disagree with your assessment of nothing good lasting. Rachel, I'm here. I'd like to take this beyond some make-out sessions and see what we might be able to create."

She opened her mouth. But froze when he shook his head.

"Before you say anything, please let me finish. I'm aware of the consequences. I'm violating professional ethics by getting involved with my client. But you've always been more than that to me. I'm willing to take the risk."

Life was nothing but unfair. Why couldn't such a man exist in New York? "I could break your heart. The few serious relationships I've been in, I've walked out of them. Heck, even Marco, although I doubt he was too heartbroken. But then there was my college—"

"I'll take that point under advisement," Colin interrupted. "But I don't think I can stop treading down this path. I've tried and failed. Frankly, I don't want to stop seeing you, despite the danger or havoc you might create in my life. You don't understand, do you? You've always been my dream girl. I thought I never had a chance. Now here you are…and you're no longer a fantasy. You're no longer the same person, but even better. You're someone I'd really like to get to know. And before you say I'm only here hitting on you because of some misguided teen crush, I hope you realize I'm a little grown-up for that. If I didn't feel a connection, I'd be elsewhere. You'd be just a client. I'd be just a lawyer. Heck, I'm not desperate for female companionship, as you indicated earlier. That's not why I'm with you."

He paced a moment. "Although I probably sound like I'm coming across as if I'm frantic. Let's postpone the rest of this conversation. Have dinner with me tomorrow night. We can get out of town, talk somewhere on neutral ground. We could fly anywhere you choose."

Chicago had been so perfect. If she went out with him again, she'd fall into bed with him. Case closed. "I don't know if that's a good idea. I've really got to think about this. You, me, together. I'm not an affair type of girl. That's all this would be."

His chin jutted forward. "Not on my part."

"Oh, Colin." She reached for him and realized her mistake the second she touched him. Her skin heated immediately. "You and I just think both still want each other. If we begin something, it could get out of control. Next weekend everyone will be at your family's Easter brunch. The whole town will have us hitched within a week."

He drew her to him. "I'd like to be hitched in the most elemental way possible. I want your skin next to mine. Maybe we'll just be a fling. But I don't think so."

He kissed her deeply. "I want you. It's that simple."

"Not tonight," Rachel managed to say shakily. Oh, Lord, she was in over her head. "Let's sleep on this. Let's…"

He nodded, recognizing he'd pushed her far enough. "Okay."

"I…" She reached for her purse and dug out her keys. "We need to lock up. Like I said, I'll have to get up early to finish the cupcakes."

"I'll make sure Libby writes you a thank-you note."

"That's not necessary," Rachel said, adjusting her ball cap.

Colin removed his apron and hung it on a peg. "Yes, it is. And Kristin will insist on it. You know my sister. She's my mother's daughter. Manners matter."

"I'm invited to a jewelry party at her house Tuesday. Heather's going and she asked me to tag along as her guest. You get a prize if you bring a friend."

"You should go. Everyone would love to see you," he said. He tugged on her apron string, loosening it.

"I never knew your sister that well. We weren't friends, since she was older." Rachel removed her apron and tossed it in the hamper.

He waited until she finished. "Age doesn't matter once you've been out in the real world for a while. Heather's your friend. You should spend time with her, get her that prize."

But spending time meant getting attached. Was that really Rachel's deepest fear? The thought struck her as she activated the alarm. The outside temperature had dropped at least another five degrees. "Looks like winter's not ready to give up the fight," she said. She pulled her coat tighter and unlocked the car.

"I heard we could have two inches of snow on Wednesday."

"Huh." The weather—now, that was a safe topic. Rachel cranked her engine, shivering a little. Unlike Colin's vehicle, hers didn't have heated seats or remote start. Her breath was visible as she began to back out. "Thank goodness home's not too far away."

"I'm fine," Colin replied, and she realized he wasn't too bothered—at least, not by the cold. Within minutes she'd parked her car in her driveway. As she'd pulled in, Colin had used his remote control to start his engine.

"Thanks for baking," he told her.

"Anytime," she said.

"I hope you mean that." He groaned and drew her to him for one last kiss. "You're already killing me. I'll see you in the morning. Think about what I said. I will."

And with that, he was gone, out into the night and through the gap in the bushes that divided the properties. Rachel shut off her engine and hurried inside. She found herself too wired to sleep, so she performed a few calming yoga poses she'd learned in a SoHo studio.

She'd call Heather sometime tomorrow, but she already knew what her friend would say. *Go for it.*

Rachel felt so confused. Questions popped into her mind as she struggled to understand what was going on. Could she just let herself totally fall for Colin? Physically, she was ready. Mentally and emotionally…? She was on the rebound. Vulnerable. She thought she was falling in love with Colin. Yet how could she trust a man after what Marco had put her through? Then again, had Colin ever let her down? She now knew how he'd truly felt in high school, and that had chased away the dark and let in the light.

Colin wasn't like Marco. But the bottom line was, Colin was her past. He was small town and happy about it. If she

let him in the door to her heart, he'd become her present.
That meant all her dreams, her enjoyment of big-city life
and her goal of owning the best bakery in Manhattan would
have to be scuttled.

Yes, the more she attempted to clear her head, the more
muddled everything became.

Chapter Eight

There was an old adage that on St. Patrick's Day everyone became Irish, and as Colin stepped out of his office at nine-thirty, he had to acknowledge that Lancaster and Morris agreed. Everywhere he glimpsed traces of "the mother country," as his very Irish paralegal, Megan O'Grady, called Ireland. He'd even succumbed himself, adding a dark green tie to accent a crisp white button-down shirt and a navy blue suit.

"You know you have that meeting with your father about the Rochester case," Megan reminded him.

"On my way there now," Colin told her, tapping the legal-size file folder he held in his hand. He glanced down at her desk, seeing the half-eaten glazed donut with green sprinkles. Kim's Diner had outdone itself today, from what he'd heard. Breakfast had had a ten-minute wait, which was an eternity in this town. Everyone was used to simply walking in and sitting down.

Lunch would also be crowded. Colin almost wished he wouldn't be missing the annual corned-beef-and-cabbage feast Kim's Diner threw every year. He only hoped the school cafeteria did as decent a job. If nothing else, the cupcakes would be delicious, should he be lucky enough to get one.

He smiled to himself. He'd gotten a kiss. That was worth much more.

"Right on time," his father greeted him as Colin entered Reginald's spacious office. Odd to think that years from now, this coveted space would be his, and Bruce would take *his* father's at the other end of the building.

At Reginald's gesture, Colin shut the door behind him and sat down in front of his father's desk. His dad stood for a second more, admiring the view of Kim's Diner, and then he settled into his oversize leather chair. "The fax regarding the Rochester settlement offer arrived as scheduled. I had a copy made for your files. I want to know what you think."

"Let me take a look." Colin reached for the paperwork and began to read. The Rochester case was something he and his father had been working on for over a year. At first Colin had been uncertain about partnering on a case with his father, but the experience had turned out to be a positive one.

"I think we can push them a bit more," Colin said as he finished reading the settlement offer. "They know they've lost the case, but they're lowballing us and trying to save their client money. They want to see if we'll go for it."

"My thought exactly. I was planning on countering with…" Reginald named a figure. "That's high enough that any counteroffer should get them into the range we believe fair compensation. If you agree, I'll have Shelley type up our response." Shelley was Reginald's paralegal.

"I agree with the decision," Colin said.

"Good." Reginald nodded, satisfied. Colin and his father

discussed a few more legal matters before his father said, "So are you heading over to Kim's for lunch? Place is going to be a madhouse today."

"Can't. I'm Libby's special guest for her school luncheon."

Reginald blinked as he remembered. "Ah, that's right. You're in charge of cupcakes, last I heard."

Colin glanced at his watch. "I'm picking them up in about twenty minutes. Rachel baked them last night and finished decorating them this morning."

"That was nice of her." His father's voice carried a questioning undertone.

"She said she did it for Libby, not me," Colin admitted.

"Sure she did," Reginald said with a small, knowing smile.

Colin attempted to remain neutral but could feel the heat under his collar. He'd thought of that kiss all night. With one touch of his lips to hers, his feelings had rushed back. He'd cared for her deeply in high school. Now he had the benefit of age. He'd dated many women and had never found the friendship or the desire he'd experienced with Rachel. If he hadn't already fallen for her, he was in grave danger of doing so. It didn't make him afraid. Only her great desire to return to New York did that.

"Speaking of Rachel, what's the status of her case?" his dad asked.

"I've received acknowledgment of our representation and I expect we'll hear more soon. I said Rachel wasn't liable for anything and demanded a few things from Marco regarding his own breach of their engagement contract. I'm also working on getting her noncompete clause reduced or removed."

"Good, good," Reginald said. "Keep me posted on further developments. Do you foresee any?"

Colin paused as he gathered up the paperwork. "What?"

"Developments."

He shook his head. "I just told you that we received a letter back."

"You can be so dense. I meant with Rachel and you," Reginald said impatiently, tapping a forefinger on the desk. "How was your client dinner? You took her flying?"

Colin didn't feel like sharing, not after last night's rejection. "It was fine."

"That's it? Surely there's more. You and I haven't had a chance to talk lately."

They hadn't. Even though he and his father had been at various business and family functions, they hadn't had any personal conversation time.

He kept the details factual. "She didn't freak out. I took her to the River Club in Chicago. She actually fell asleep on the flight there. Food was great and the evening gave us a chance to clear the air about some things that happened in high school. We had a misunderstanding about prom. She thought I was taking her and I thought she was joking."

"And you went with someone else—who, I don't remember. So what else?" Reginald prompted.

"And that's it," Colin said, closing the file folder. "Rachel's planning to go back to New York at some point. She's not staying here. Even if I wanted anything to develop, it's not possible."

"So you do want something to develop?" Reginald rose and paced a little.

His father was one of the best cross-examiners in the state. "I don't know what healthy red-blooded male wouldn't, except maybe her ex, and he still claims he wants her back," Colin replied. "But I'm starting to realize it's useless to try to make anything permanent happen between us. Tell Mom not to get her hopes up. I know you both think it's high time I settled down."

"Oh." His father seemed extremely disappointed in the news. "You can't change Rachel's mind?"

"About what?"

"Leaving? Dating you? I don't know." Reginald appeared exasperated, a rare state for a man usually in complete control. "You tell me. You're crazy about her. Always have been. We all love her. You two would be perfect together. Everyone agrees."

"Dad." Colin shook his head in an attempt to ward off additional questions. "She and I are two different people who now live two different lives. We're also both grown-ups. Let us work through this nonexistent relationship thing on our own. She's my client. I've already crossed that line. She's very worried that all of Morrisville will have us hitched within the week."

Reginald tilted his head, conceding that point. "Client aside, she's also your friend. You've been emotionally involved since grade school. I'm not going to split hairs about blurring professional lines or ethics. That's the least of my concerns. I probably haven't said this enough, but I only want you to be happy."

"I know." Colin did. He'd been a typical teenager, and at around age sixteen, he'd started thinking that suddenly his parents had grown extremely stupid and hadn't understood him anymore. He'd pretty much maintained that attitude until his midtwenties. Not until these past few years had he begun forging a new relationships with his dad, moving from that of parent and child to that of man-to-man and friend-to-friend. The change was good.

"Well, let me know if there's anything I can do to help," Reginald said, ending the conversation.

"I will." Colin stood, having gathered up all the legal documents. "I'm off to get the cupcakes and meet Libby. I'll deal with the rest of this later today."

"Tomorrow's not too late. Don't rush Libby or anything else. It's a holiday. At least enjoy a little bit of the day."

"I will." Colin exited his father's office and soon had deposited everything on his own desk. Then he went into the men's washroom, checked his appearance and headed out the door.

"Hey, Colin!"

Colin pivoted to find his best friend standing down the hall. "Hey! Bruce! I didn't know you were back!"

"We arrived late last night," Bruce explained. "I know I wasn't supposed to return to the office until tomorrow, but I was itching to get back to work. My desk is a mess. Besides, this gets me out of Christina's hair. She's nesting or something. Scrubbing the kitchen down, although she just cleaned everything before we left."

Colin shook his head and laughed. "My sisters were a bit odd during their pregnancies, too. Kristin painted five rooms, and not one of them was the nursery. She claims that type of behavior is normal." Bruce laughed at that.

"So, did I miss anything while I was gone? The receptionist said some girl came in looking for me, but she didn't leave her name."

Possessiveness gripped Colin. "It was Rachel, but I've got her case."

Bruce shifted his weight to his left foot. Since he was technically still on vacation, he wore a long-sleeved green

Henley and blue Dockers. "Rachel needed a lawyer?" he asked.

"Yeah." Colin glanced at his watch. "Listen, not to cut you off, but I have to run over to Libby's school. I'm her guest at their feast today. Can we catch up later?"

Bruce nodded. "Let's. Are you available tonight? I could do an early dinner. Bella has Girl Scouts or something and Christina will be busy."

Yeah, Colin was free. Rachel had rejected his offer for food. "How does five at the country club sound?"

"Perfect," Bruce said. "Meet you there."

The two men separated, and soon Colin had crossed the parking lot and the street and entered Kim's Diner. Even though the breakfast had ended and the lunch hour hadn't started, the place remained packed.

"Hey, Colin," Kim greeted him as she passed a customer's order to a waitress. "I'm assuming you're here for your cupcakes."

"Yes," Colin said, scanning the diner for Rachel.

"Don't bother looking. She's not here. She looked like crud, almost like she's getting a cold. I sent her home an hour ago. But I've got Libby's cupcakes. They're cute. Rachel did a fantastic job."

Kim disappeared into the kitchen and returned carrying two white paperboard containers. She set the boxes on the counter and opened the lids. The cupcakes had perfectly piped green frosting crowning them, and Rachel had indeed covered the swirled frosting with green and white sprinkles. "I hope Libby likes them," Kim said.

"I'm sure she will," Colin said as Kim closed the lids. He already knew how delicious the frosting was and he had no doubt the confections would be sweet sensations. He wasn't certain how much a class of second graders would appreciate Rachel's fine culinary effort, but he knew he was thankful for all that Rachel had put in, especially if she was coming down with a cold. He frowned as the implications struck him. Their late night had probably contributed to her being run-down.

Cupcakes in hand, Colin made his way to Libby's school. Lunchtime found him having fun, despite sitting on those tiny elementary-school chairs that brought adult knees almost up to the chest. Libby's twin sister, Maggie, had invited her grandmother, so Colin saw his mother before the entire event ended and he headed back to his car.

He climbed into the Aura and glanced at the clock. Not quite 1:00 p.m. He had plenty of time, he instantly decided. Everyone at the law firm would be taking a long, corned-beef-and-cabbage lunch at Kim's. No one would be in a hurry to return to work, and not much would get done at Lancaster and Morris the rest of the day. That was why his father had said tomorrow was early enough to get the response out on the Rochester case.

So instead of heading back to the office, Colin drove his car in the opposite direction and retraced the path Rachel had driven last night.

SHE WAS GOING to kill whoever was making that awful racket. The pounding was enough to wake up the dead, which was exactly how she looked, Rachel noted with a grimace as she passed the hallway mirror. She could see a shadow of some-one through the stained-glass inset in the front door.

"Hold your horses," she called, shuffling the few extra feet. She turned the handle and opened the door to reveal the perpetrator, Colin Morris.

He was shivering, as if he'd been out in the forty-degree weather awhile. "Did I wake you?"

Rachel stared at him, her jaw dropping. "No. I always look like this." A blast of cold air swirled around her bare feet; she'd left her slippers upstairs. "In or out. It's cold and I'm freezing."

"Tell me about it," Colin said, stepping forward. "I've been enjoying the weather out here for over five minutes. Your doorbell doesn't work."

"Hasn't for years. You could have walked in. The door's never locked." Rachel padded her way to the sitting room, where her grandmother kept an afghan on the couch. She sat down and wrapped the blanket protectively around her, taking extra care to cover her feet.

"Libby loved the cupcakes. Thank you. They were a big hit with her classmates." Colin followed her and hovered nearby.

Rachel yawned. "Good. So it's afternoon already?"

"A little after one," Colin replied. He sat on a chair perpendicular to the sofa she was on. "Kim told me you weren't feeling well so I decided to check on you."

"I'm fine, really. Just tired," Rachel admitted. "I've been going at top speed since mid-February and my body is starting to rebel. It doesn't want to bake all the Easter cakes I've got to make this week. Says it wants time off."

"You have to take better care of yourself," Colin said, sincerity evident. He removed his coat and laid it over the arm of the chair.

"I'm trying," Rachel said. She stretched her neck and then paused as she realized that Colin had shown up on her doorstep. "Don't worry about me. I took my temperature and I don't have a fever. And no sniffles. No congestion. Simple fatigue. I'm going to start taking vitamin supplements tonight. My mother said she'd pick some up on the way home."

"I could run out and get them for you," he offered. "What do you need?"

She curled her feet closer to her. "That's sweet, but a few hours won't make a difference. Like I said, I've just worn myself down. You can only go so far before stress catches up with you."

"True," Colin agreed. "Which means that from here on out, you must relax more. As your lawyer and your friend, I insist on it."

She studied him. She was about to ask, *And what will you do if I don't?* but the question died on her tongue. She'd never seen such intense concern before—at least, not directed toward her. "Okay," she said, caving in.

"You're not going to fight me on this?" He seemed surprised, and for the first time she noticed his green tie.

The corners of her lips inched upward. "No. Even I'm not that radical. I know when to fold my hand. This is my health. Exhausting myself sabotages my goal of starting my business and getting back to New York."

"Exactly," Colin agreed, although he appeared uncomfortable with the latter part of her assertion. "If you're sick, who will bake all the cakes for Easter? I'd help, but you remember how useful I was last night."

She smiled at this. "You managed to sift the flour. I'm sure that with some training you could be tolerable in the kitchen. Even top chefs have had to start somewhere." She laughed as he made a sour face at her and stuck out his tongue.

He leaned forward. "Are you hungry? I might not be a cook, but I can at least find things in the kitchen, especially if you want something. Have you eaten anything?"

"Not since early this morning. I came home and fell asleep," Rachel admitted.

"You need to eat. What can I get you?" Colin stood. "No excuses. I'm already on my feet."

Colin's sincerity was sweet and she gave in. His concern was touching. He shed his suit coat and rolled up the sleeves on his white dress shirt. "There's some leftover broccoli-cheese soup in the refrigerator. Second shelf. You just have to reheat it. About one minute on high."

"One thing you should learn about me is that I'm the king of the microwave. I can warm up anything. Be right back."

He was gone about five minutes, and Rachel used the time to close her eyes and simply rest. She hadn't realized until this morning how physically deflated she was. She'd had to drag herself out of bed to finish Libby's cupcakes. She hadn't minded the work, but she'd found herself unmotivated. As if she needed a vacation from her vacation. Not that moving back to Morrisville had been a picnic. Hardly. If anything, the man now out of sight in the kitchen had compounded her stress.

One thing was for certain. If nothing else, Colin's reappearance in her life had opened her eyes to the fact that she'd deluded herself about Marco. She'd escaped to New York, only to trap herself in a false dream.

Now, Colin… The man oozed excitement. Just seeing him on her doorstep had sent a thrill through her. He'd come because he cared, not because her being AWOL from work had caused him any type of distress. Marco worried only about the appearance of the person. Colin worried about the person.

Which was probably a good thing, Rachel thought ruefully as she touched the top of her head. Her hair was a bird's nest of tangles. She didn't have any makeup on. She hadn't brushed her teeth since this morning. She surely reeked of both cupcakes and simmering cabbage—not a pleasant combination.

But Colin didn't seem to mind. There he was, dressed in pants she knew had cost a pretty penny, carrying a tray of steaming-hot soup. "I found some crackers in the pantry and brought you a glass of orange juice. That's supposed to help, isn't it? I remember my mother always forcing me to drink at least a gallon when I was younger and she believed I was catching some deadly virus."

"OJ has vitamin C in it," Rachel said as Colin set down the tray. He'd even added a small vase and a flower, which she knew he'd lifted from the center of the kitchen table.

He glanced at the adornment and he chuckled. "Well, every commercial on television shows some sort of foliage. This was the easiest thing."

"It's a thoughtful touch," Rachel said, for there were no other words to describe his sincere gesture. He'd just risen in her estimation a thousandfold. She sighed and exhaled on her soupspoon to cool the contents. This change in Colin was wonderful. Yet this moment would make leaving him all the harder. Despite herself, she could easily fall in love with Colin. She'd cared for him all her life, but the man he'd become made him even more endearing. The grown-up Colin Morris was everything she ever could have hoped for in a mate.

And everything she'd walked away from when she'd fled Morrisville after high school. The bitter irony assailed her, proving perhaps she'd been a lot more foolish than she cared to admit. She busied herself with eating the soup and encouraged Colin to tell her the entire story of Libby's lunch. Anything to keep her mind off the truth she'd just realized.

"So was Elmer already in his spot when you went by the diner?" she asked. "He and Harold have been sitting next to each other at the counter for years, and my mom told me that on St. Patrick's Day they show up at dawn and don't leave until the last person clears out. She says they eat and argue all day. Not that they don't see each other all the time, but for some reason today's different. And the diner doesn't even serve alcohol!"

"I didn't notice," Colin revealed. "I was more worried about you and being on time to Libby's event. My mom was Maggie's guest and she got one of your cupcakes. Said it was delicious."

"I'm glad the lunch went well." The hall clock chimed two. Had he really been here almost an hour? "You're missing work! I'm going to get you in trouble!"

He laughed and shook his head. "My tardiness won't matter. Today everyone's Irish and taking an extended lunch. We'll all be pious again by Friday."

"Seems so weird when St. Patrick's Day and Good Friday are in the same week. Start with a party, end with Stations of the Cross. Church—that's where my mother will be. Even Kim will join her for evening service."

Colin leaned forward as if to hear her better. "Not you?"

She shrugged. "I may go this year, if only to please them. Going to church hasn't been on my to-do list. Marco and I didn't attend except to get the church scheduled for the wedding. But I've agreed to go with them on Easter Sunday. We'll do that, and then have brunch at your parents'. Tradition, you know."

He rose and reached for the tray "I know. I haven't missed going to church or brunch once in thirty-one years."

"You *are* thirty-one," Rachel pointed out.

He stood there with a grin. "Exactly. I'm sure I was there in the womb, too. Funny, how time passes and some things stay the same."

"Okay, we're not exactly old, but today I feel it, so be careful. I'll be thirty—"

"April fifteenth," Colin finished for her. "I think of you every tax day. It makes your birthday easy to remember."

"Yay," Rachel quipped sarcastically. "I'm sure most people don't associate my aging with anything pleasant."

"Well, I do. I usually get a refund. I file early and feel sorry for those who wait until the last minute." He shifted his weight, balancing the tray.

"That's usually me," Rachel acknowledged. "I hate doing taxes."

"Now, how did I know that?" He smiled again, making himself even more charming than usual. "I'm going to get out of your hair, let you get some much-needed rest. Let me put this stuff in the kitchen."

"Thanks. Just leave everything on the counter by the sink. I'll either get it or someone will. You've already done enough. I'll clean up."

"If you're sure. I'm pretty good at loading a dishwasher."

"I'm positive," Rachel said, watching as Colin left the room. Then she stretched out her feet and wiggled her toes. She'd worn green nail polish in honor of the holiday. Polish on her toenails was a silly little thing, but since a cook had to stand in sensible, closed-toe shoes during her shift, Rachel had long ago taken to wearing funky-colored nail polish as her little secret. She tucked her feet back under the afghan as Colin returned.

"I'll catch up with you tomorrow," he said. "I'm having dinner with Bruce at the country club. He and Christina are back in town and he's free tonight. I hardly see him now that he's married and a stepfather, so we're going to hang out."

Rachel nodded. "Tell him I said hi. Tell him I'm going to be busy all week. I have orders for over twenty-five coconut cakes, including one for your mother's brunch. That's thirty coconuts I have to drain."

He frowned. "You don't use the packaged stuff?"

She made a face. "Absolutely not, and you'll taste why Sunday."

Colin shrugged into his suit coat. "Okay. After those cupcakes I have no doubt you're an expert. So is Bruce, so I'm going to pick his brain on your case a little, find out what he thinks."

"If you think that's necessary," Rachel said. "I'm certain you've got a pretty good handle on it."

He seemed pleased by her compliment. "Thanks. I appreciate your vote of confidence."

"I only hire the best," Rachel said, her words causing a wry smile to split Colin's face.

"As do I. Those cupcakes were the prize item. I'll talk to you tomorrow. And don't work yourself up too much over those cakes. You're not in this alone. I'm sure you could recruit any help you need. We're all here for you." He buttoned his overcoat.

She nodded. "I'm starting to realize that and it's a bit overwhelming. Now, go. Goodness knows if my mother and grandmother find you here, there will be fifty million questions for me to answer. I'm trying to destress, not go deeper into distress."

"Yes, ma'am." Colin mock saluted and soon Rachel heard the door shut behind him. She leaned back against the sofa. He'd spent part of his afternoon with her. He'd cooked her soup—okay, reheated it, but still. His kindness spoke volumes. He hadn't tried to kiss her. He'd done nothing but simply *be* with her and keep her company.

She'd liked it.

A lot.

COLIN STAYED BUSY with work until he met Bruce at the Morrisville Country Club. His friend was already in the bar, nursing the only drink he'd have all evening, a fine Scotch served on the rocks.

"Think I'll join you in having one of those," Colin said, gesturing to the bartender.

"If you're only going to drink one, might as well make it the best," Bruce agreed.

"Rachel was saying something along those lines today," Colin said, taking a seat on the leather-backed bar stool. He'd checked his coat.

"How is Rachel? You mentioned you're doing some legal work for her."

"I am." Colin had just enough time to apprise Bruce of the situation before the hostess arrived to tell them their table was ready. The bartender returned with Colin's drink, and he held it aloft as he and Bruce made their way into the main dining room.

"If you were in my shoes, what might you do about Rachel's case? Have any thoughts or suggestions?" Colin asked, setting his menu aside. He knew the contents by heart, and tonight's special, no surprise, was corned beef, cabbage, new potatoes and Irish soda bread.

"There are a few intellectual-property cases that set legal precedent." Colin took a sip of his Scotch whiskey as Bruce began to recall some current case law. Bruce's mind could remember even the smallest details, and by the time their entrées arrived, Colin had an idea for dealing with Marco and his attorneys.

"So how are you and Rachel doing otherwise?" Bruce asked casually.

"What do you mean?" Colin asked, feigning indifference. He knew exactly what information his friend was digging for, but it was somewhere in the guy code that he pretend otherwise.

Bruce sipped his drink. "I don't know. You've always had the hots for the girl and she's back in town. You tell me what's going on."

"Her stay is only temporary," Colin hedged.

Bruce was not to be daunted. "Sounds ideal. That's usually about the perfect relationship length for you." Bruce pointed a forefinger at Colin as if to say *Gotcha.*

"Ha." Colin faked a laugh. "Hardly."

"Shall I name some of them? Right before I met Christina, there was…" He snapped his fingers. "Gina, I think. Then that Miss Indiana. I'm sure you remember that New Year's Eve fiasco. I still can't keep count of all your revolving-door relationships."

"You are such a card. See me laugh," Colin said, swallowing some of the corned beef. He wasn't sure what the country-club chefs did, but the meat here was never tough and always tender.

"I'm being serious. Nothing or no one sticks to you."

"Only because I haven't wanted anything or anyone to stick. Weren't you always the one in college who described women like running shoes? You try them on, but since you only need one good pair, you find the keeper."

"Not exactly my quote, but close enough," Bruce said. "So I didn't date seriously until I met Christina. I didn't lead anyone on."

"We're two lawyers whose conversation is about to go in endless circles," Colin protested. "As for Rachel, she's returning to New York once her case settles. Even if we can't get her out of her noncompete, she can work anywhere after six months. That's the maximum she'll be here until she flies the coop again. She's a big-city girl now. No more Podunkville for her."

"You still like her, don't you?" Bruce said, savoring another sip of Scotch.

"Terribly," Colin admitted, not telling Bruce that his feelings for Rachel already went beyond that. "I thought I could be professional, but I'm more attracted to her now than I was in high school. Especially since…"

"Since what? Don't stop." Bruce waved his fork, prodding Colin to finish his sentence.

"I learned the truth the other night. She and I talked. You were right. She never liked you. It was always me who she preferred."

"I knew it," Bruce said triumphantly. Then he put another bite of potatoes in his mouth and digested the implications of Colin's words. "How did you find this out?"

"She told me."

"Yeah, you said that. What was the impetus behind the conversation?"

"I took her to dinner. Flew her to Chicago. The River

Club. She wanted to clear the air. She didn't want anyone getting the wrong idea or playing matchmaker. We both realized we'd been thinking the wrong things all these years."

Bruce leaned back in his chair. "So this is where it gets complicated. She liked you—you liked her—neither of you knew it. And now that you've cleared the air…" Bruce paused for a second as Colin nodded in confirmation. "Now both of you have these feelings that haven't changed. If anything else, they're stronger because you're consenting adults."

"And she's not staying and I'm not leaving. Kind of ruins anything before it starts. I don't want a one-night or two-week stand thing with her. She's worth much more than that."

Bruce set his napkin on the edge of the table. "You know, I never thought I'd see this day again."

Colin's brow creased. "You're not making sense. St. Patrick's Day comes every year."

"Yeah, but you being tortured by a woman doesn't. You were always mooning over Rachel. You pined for her. And she's back, and you're moping again. You've got it pretty bad. You've never been like this over anyone else."

"And it sucks," Colin said, not brothering to disagree. "None of this is pleasant at all. My stomach's in knots. I'm spouting clichés." He winced.

"I wish I knew what to tell you," Bruce said. He'd managed to clean his plate.

Colin glanced down. Half his food remained. He'd lost his appetite. "I don't think there are any answers. I think I solve her legal problems and let her go. End of story."

"Seems a shame," Bruce said.

"Star-crossed lovers. Only we aren't lovers. Dramatic irony or something like that. I only got a C in English, but I understand my role in this. Whoever would have thought that?" He never had, that was for sure.

"On a happier note, you're closer than ever to getting your plane," Bruce pointed out.

Owning his own plane. His huge dream. Colin focused on that. "And trust me, I'm counting down the days. We hear we take delivery Monday, March 31. The company reps are flying it in and staying for two days of hands-on training."

"I want to be one of the first guests to go up with you—once you know what you are doing," Bruce declared, staking his claim.

"Absolutely." Colin nodded. Bruce had always supported Colin's flying habit, so he didn't correct Bruce and tell him he was already certified on the aircraft, which was why they'd chosen it. "We've just about ironed out our usage agreement. Accommodating four ownership schedules is a little tricky, but we're pretty close."

"I guess you have to make it equitable."

"That plus whoever flies more should, logically, pay more. That's probably me. I'm the only single one in the group. I'll use the plane a lot."

"You could always fly to New York and visit Rachel," Bruce suggested.

Colin pushed his plate aside, giving up on dinner entirely. "She already dismissed that idea," Colin replied. "It's like New York is her territory and she's afraid of trespassers."

"Someone else will come along," Bruce said, although both men knew the words really weren't any kind of consolation.

"I never thought I was missing anything until Rachel

came home," Colin said as the waiter whisked his plate away, then returned a few moments later with a carryout box. "Both she and I acknowledge there's something between us here, but exploring it would be awkward. Her family and mine go too far back. It would be too weird to see each other after everything ended. She's already baking my mom coconut cake with real coconut. Like, she has to break the shell open to get the meat out."

"Coconut?" Bruce's eyes gleamed. "That's one of my favorites."

"Well, Rachel is bringing a cake to brunch on Sunday, so you better move to get a slice and tell your wife. Rachel's stuff will go fast. You snooze and you'll lose."

"I'll make sure I'm first in line." He laughed at Colin's expression. "Second. Right behind you."

The waiter approached and Bruce waved off the offer of dessert. "Just the check, please."

"She'll be baking those cakes all week. She was home resting today. I'm worried about her. She looked tired."

"So stop by the diner and help her out. I'm sure there's something you can do."

Colin thought back to baking the cupcakes. "Not certain that's wise," he said, recalling the kiss. Pleasurable, yes, but not a smart idea if they were to remain "just friends."

"Well, keep me posted on both your love life and her case. If I can help out with either, let me know."

"Thanks…I think."

Bruce took the leather holder from the waiter. "I'll buy this round. You get the next," he told Colin.

"Okay." Colin replied, reciprocating Bruce's grin. The country club sent the law firm a bill at the end of the month. Each partner had a generous food allowance, so Lancaster and Morris was really the one paying for dinner. Colin felt little guilt over the entitlement; he and Bruce had discussed legal business, after all.

Within the next ten minutes, Colin found himself driving home. He parked his car in the garage of his ranch house and entered. The place was depressingly silent. Normally, he didn't mind, but the idea struck him that maybe he ought to get a cat. Fish, perhaps. Those were pretty simple to care for. Just toss in a few fish flakes once a day and keep the water pH regulated. At least there'd be something waiting for him.

He clicked on the plasma TV. The sounds of a basketball game flooded the room and chased away the ensuing doldrums.

He kicked off his shoes and settled down on the couch. She'd gotten under his skin, darn it. She was all he thought about. Talking about Rachel to Bruce had helped, but the conversation still hadn't allowed Colin to shed his own stress, which was increasing daily. He'd work out for at least two hours tomorrow, but doubted that the karate he'd practice or the weights he'd lift would clear his mind or soothe his soul.

Colin had always been a problem solver. He liked being a detective, finding solutions to things others missed.

With Rachel, he was drawing a complete blank.

Chapter Nine

"So, are you glad you came?" Heather asked about fifteen minutes into the home-jewelry party Rachel had agreed to attend.

"Yes, you were right," Rachel admitted to her friend. She lifted a glass of wine as she wove her way through Kristin's kitchen and stopped at a table covered with food. "I'm glad you dragged me to this. I thought it would be... Well, I was wrong."

"Of course you were." Heather laughed. "These home parties aren't cheesy. They're a fun excuse to get together, do a little shopping and eat a lot."

"I could do without the eating part," Rachel said, snagging a celery stick and taking a bite. "I've put on two pounds since I came home. I'm not sure why. I used to work at a restaurant and eat pasta all the time."

"You're stressed," Heather said knowingly. "I read that tension can add ten pounds. Something to do with the adrenal gland."

"Stressed is just desserts spelled backward," Rachel said.

"Clever. In my case, it's all baby weight. In your case, it's simply nerves. How many coconuts did you do?"

"Way too many." Rachel laughed. "The guy at the supermarket in Batesville told me I was loco. I bought every coconut they had and still needed to drive into Greensburg for the rest. It's not like the food distributors around here stock coconuts in the quantity I required."

"I just use the flaked stuff in that blue package." Heather began to fill her plate with a sample of everything from chips and dips to brownies. "I don't know how you managed. How do you even crack one?"

"You drill a hole, drain the milk and then bake the shell. That makes it easier to crack when you hit it with a mallet. Then you scoop out the inside."

"So are you done?" Heather asked.

"I wish. I still have a lot to do before Saturday. My grandmother took over baking some of the regular diner staples this week. That's helped out. I'm still baking five-dozen bear claws a day, though. She's not about to pick those anytime soon. Too sticky. Although I modified her recipe. More taste and less mess."

Heather added carrot sticks to her plate. "You need to load up and not just eat one thing at a time," she told Rachel.

"I'm good," Rachel answered. Meaning she was fine on food. Heather had deliberately misconstrued her words.

"I'm not so sure about that, but I bet I know someone who'd like to find out."

"Don't go there," Rachel warned. "Not where Kristin could overhear anything you say."

"What—is there some good gossip being spilled over here?" Kristin asked as she moved to add more crackers to a tray.

"Colin's still got a crush on Rachel," Heather announced.

Rachel momentarily closed her eyes as her jaw dropped open. "Heather!"

"It's okay. We've all known that. That's old news," Kristin said, as if that made everything better.

Rachel wished the floor would open up and swallow her. Unfortunately, it was too early to bow out gracefully from the party and go home. "Great. Everyone in town's probably been talking about me."

"Yeah, and most of them are here," Heather teased.

"And I wasn't coming to this party tonight. Why did I change my mind?" Rachel asked. She reached for a small piece of brownie and popped the chocolate in her mouth. Yep, stress made you eat. Big-time.

"Ah, don't let Heather here scare you away," Kristin teased. "You know we can't take her anywhere. Besides, my mother's the busybody. She's been raving for a week about the Easter cake you're bringing Sunday. I think she wants to hook you up with my brother just so he doesn't starve. The man can't cook a bit."

Rachel remembered the incident with the flour, and her face heated. Kristin didn't seem to notice as she continued, "Mom's the one you have to worry about, so I would try to avoid sitting by her."

Kristin finished loading the cracker tray. "I myself believe my brother's an idiot and any woman would be a fool to take him on. Here, let me get you some more wine. You're just about empty. If this is only your first glass, you definitely need a refill."

Kristin took Rachel's glass and made away with it, empty cracker box in her other hand. "I'm going to kill you later," Rachel promised Heather.

Heather had the gall to smirk. "No, you won't. You love

me too much and have missed getting grief from people who care about you. Your life in New York has been stodgy. I'm making it my mission to liven it up. Besides, Kristin's married to a shrink. She's using reverse psychology on her brother and you. I use the technique on Keith all the time. Works wonders."

"Great." Rachel's sarcasm was obvious.

At that moment a group of five girls, two of them twins, raced into the room and grabbed plates. "Mom, she's butting!" one of them shouted.

"Cut it out and take turns!" Kristin hollered.

"I am so not ready for this next phase of my life," Rachel said as one of the young girls accidentally jostled her.

Heather grinned at Rachel's discomfort. She'd left Erin at home with her husband, who was probably enjoying the semifreedom. "Sure you are. Now, let's go look at the jewelry. Moms like the reasonable stuff since grimy little hands grab it all the time. This company guarantees everything. I've returned one or two things and never had a problem."

"We're not going to play any of those silly games, are we?" Rachel asked, succumbing and taking a plate and covering it with veggies.

"That's at the basket party. Beware, you get on our party circuit and you'll get hit up for candles, too. Now, those you can really use. Light a few and let the magic happen."

"I'm going to remove your entrails. I'm trained to use knives. I know how to do it. You should see me bone a chicken," Rachel said.

"So not listening," Heather chanted, leading the way into the large family room. Rachel found herself sitting between Heather and Colin's mother as the home-party lady began displaying her wares. Kristin brought Rachel a refilled glass of wine and Rachel sipped the liquid gratefully.

She knew most of the people present, but others were more recent Morrisville transplants. All but Rachel were married, yet no one seemed to mind or care about Rachel's single status. Even better, no one mentioned Colin or fixing her up with a brother or some divorcé they knew at work.

She hadn't socialized exclusively with women, if you didn't count her mother and grandmother, in ages. She'd never spent much time with Marco's sisters. They'd liked her, but they hadn't made much of an effort to do things with their future sister-in-law. *And they were to be my bridesmaids,* Rachel realized ruefully. Funny how she was more comfortable with the people from Morrisville, Indiana, who thought rings from some home-party catalog were pretty high-fashion stuff.

Rachel studied the various rings on display, which were at least made with fourteen-carat gold. Suddenly, one caught her attention. The ring was woven gold in a simple floral design, but Rachel fell instantly in love with both the ring and its forty-dollar price tag.

Why not, she said to herself. The jewelry from Marco that she hadn't sold she'd put in her mother's safe-deposit box. She had no idea what to do with the various pieces, which were gaudy and worth hundreds. She also had no place to wear them and out of sight was out of mind.

"You should get that," Heather said as Rachel tried the display model on her left hand.

"I don't know. It's not like I wear jewelry when I bake. I'm also trying to save up. It seems like too much of an indulgence. I'm getting used to my hand being bare again," Rachel said as her second thoughts started.

"Live a little," Heather encouraged her. "Tell you what. Put that ring on my ticket and I'll buy half. Consider it an early birthday present."

"Oh, no," Rachel said, shaking her head as she realized the implications. "You are not getting me a present or throwing me a party."

"Never said that," Heather responded as she tried on a necklace.

"Maybe not, but I know you," Rachel insisted. "I'm turning thirty. You would do something like that."

"I might. Thirty is a milestone," Heather admitted with a guilty expression. "I've been thinking about hosting a small gathering around April 15."

"Don't," Rachel warned. "I'm not in a partying mood."

"Fine," Heather said, removing the necklace and reaching for another one. "But no matter what, you are purchasing that ring."

In the end, Rachel caved and bought the ring. However, she paid for her only item herself. "You should receive your purchase in about three weeks," the party consultant said as she handed Rachel her receipt.

"Thanks." Rachel stood. Checkout was in the dining room and she'd just survived her first American home-sales party unscathed. Already someone else waited behind Rachel to order the items she'd selected.

"Hey, Rachel," Kristin called into the room. "Would you be able to take Mom home? She doesn't drive at night and I'm not going to be able to get out of here for a while yet."

"Sure," Rachel agreed. "Do you want me to take her now?"

"Whenever you're leaving is fine. No hurry," Kristin replied.

Less then ten minutes later, Rachel drove Loretta Morris home. She pulled into the Morris driveway, right behind a silver Aura.

"Oh, Colin's here. He must have come to see his father. They're working on a case together. You'll have to step inside and say hello."

Rachel recognized she was being set up, but before she could decline, Loretta was already out the passenger door and halfway up the walk. The motion sensors caught her movements and light flooded the yard.

"Mom? Is that you?" Colin walked through the front door and onto the porch. "Hi, Rachel. What are you doing here? Mom, I thought I was to pick you up if you wanted to leave early."

"With the price of gas what it is, that would be silly," Loretta said, pointing. "Rachel was driving this way. She lives right next door, you know."

"How well I do." Colin stepped off the porch and gave his mother a kiss as she passed by. He walked over to where Rachel waited, protected only by her driver's door.

"I think we've been set up," she said.

The corners of Colin's lips inched upward into a grin. "Looks like. But it's okay. I needed to talk with you anyway. Running into you makes things convenient. Marco's attorneys answered my letter. I was going to call you tomorrow and arrange a meeting so we could discuss their response and what to send back to them."

A tremor of fear gripped her. "Is it bad?"

"It's not what we'd hoped for, but certainly not the end of the world," Colin said easily, as if he had few worries about dealing with her case.

"It's nerve-racking for me," she admitted.

"I understand. That's the hard thing about negotiations. You have to be patient. You come from opposite ends and meet somewhere in the middle. We'll end up where we want. Trust me."

Somehow, she did. He was a professional and he wouldn't steer her wrong. He was on her side. She nodded.

"So you had fun tonight?" he asked.

The words slipped out. "I bought a ring."

"Ah. Fingers feeling a little naked."

She shook her head, the desire for companionship overriding her urge to leave. "I'm not sure if I was simply caught up in the moment or what, but I really like the ring. The party lady said I'd receive it in about three weeks. I hope I still want it then."

He was more confident. "You will. Can I ask how much you spent?"

"Forty. Plus tax. Shipping. So it was about forty-six something altogether. I probably shouldn't have."

He chuckled. "An occasional urge to be irresponsible is normal. I'm glad you let go a little. This whole thing with Marco and moving home has you uptight. You are feeling better than yesterday, right?"

She nodded and stepped out from behind her door. "Absolutely. My grandmother's taking on some of the baking this week to help out. Tomorrow's going to be a big day, as is Thursday. Everyone's going to church Friday, since it's Good Friday, so I'm doing all the icing that day. Pickup is Saturday. The diner will be crazy."

"So should we talk about the case now?" He glanced at his illuminated watch. "It's only nine. When are you due at the diner?"

"Actually, I'm off. Kim banned me from arriving until one. I left enough bear claws for everyone to get their fix."

"So you don't have to turn in right away." He'd edged closer to her.

"No, I'm all right. We could talk now if that's what you're suggesting. That might be a good idea, because I doubt I could sleep worrying about what's in that letter they sent."

"Then let's get out of here and head over to my place. I brought your file home so I could work on it tonight."

She'd never seen his house. She hesitated, deliberating.

"It's not as cold as yesterday, but I'm not wearing a coat—it's inside," Colin said, prodding her gently to make a decision.

"I'll follow you in my car," Rachel said. That was safer. By driving to his place in her own vehicle, she could leave whenever she wanted and not rely on Colin to take her home.

"That will be fine," he said. "Do you want to come in and say hello to Dad?"

She shook her head. "Do you think he'll mind if I skip it? I'll see him Sunday."

"He'll be okay with it. He's watching one of those made-for-TV movies. Let me get my coat and be right out," Colin said, disappearing.

By the time he returned, Rachel had backed her car up, giving Colin enough room to easily do the same. He led the way to a newer part of town, a subdivision of middle-class homes built about ten years earlier. She knew which house because a garage door was going up, and within seconds he'd parked his car inside and was waiting for her to pull into his driveway.

"Home sweet home. Come on in," he said as she stepped out.

She followed him through the garage and into a small laundry room. Then they entered his kitchen. The entire house was clean and devoid of decorating essentials.

"It's nice. Tidy," Rachel hedged. His house was, in a word, *bland*.

He laughed at her fake compliment. "Oh, don't hold back. Be honest. My sisters call the place institutional. I'm afraid the next time one of them gets pregnant, she'll come over and paint the entire place."

"Everything is pretty beige," Rachel admitted. "The house could be really nice, though, if you fixed it up."

He shrugged. "It's a starter home. Nothing fancy. Picked it up during the last housing downturn for a steal. Needs a woman's touch, but so far I've fended off my sisters by telling them I'm broke. I'll tell them my excess money goes toward two priorities—my retirement fund and my plane payment. I'm never home much anyway."

"As long as you're satisfied. That's what counts." She glanced around his kitchen. Basic oak cabinets. Linoleum in a nondescript design. Those laminate countertops everyone had if they couldn't afford Corian or granite. The kitchen did have one major plus—lots of space to cook.

"The only room I've personalized is this way," Colin said, leading her into the vaulted great room. Here he'd splurged on an overstuffed sectional sofa, huge plasma-screen television and some aerial airplane photographs that she soon learned he'd taken while flying.

"How long have you lived here?" she asked, settling into

a corner of the beige sofa, which was bare of any accent pillows.

"Couple of years. I rented an apartment before that. Your file is in my office. Let me get it. While I'm at it, would you like anything to drink?"

She hadn't realized she was thirsty until he'd mentioned refreshment. "Water, please."

"I've got other things, too," he suggested.

"Your sister plied me with two glasses of wine. Water would be perfect."

"Then that's what I'll serve." Colin returned a few minutes later balancing two filled glasses and a file folder. Rachel had turned on the TV. Now she clicked the off button, plunging the screen into darkness.

"You can leave that on."

She shifted, reaching for the glass he held out. "I'd rather not. Then I won't be able to concentrate on the matter at hand."

He laughed. "So you still stare at it the way you did when we were kids?"

One of her worst habits. "Yes. When a good show is on, it commands my attention. It's like I'm hypnotized. In my apartment I only had a nineteen-inch screen. Figured the best way not to watch TV was to buy one of the smaller sizes. Even with hundreds of channels, I'll find myself fixated on any type of cooking show."

He sat near her, but not touching. "I don't watch many shows. I like the noise factor. I'll have the TV on even when I'm not in the room. I've discovered I don't like silence."

"I'm the opposite. My job is so chaotic and noisy that I want my apartment to be still and serene. Although, New York is never quiet. You hear car horns and other noises

24/7. I've actually had some trouble falling asleep since I've come home. It's almost too quiet."

She sat there a moment, pondering their differences. "So what do you have for me?"

He removed an envelope from the file folder and handed it to her. "Here's the latest letter. In essence, they're still maintaining your recipes were works for hire and belong to them. They are willing to drop their claim, however, for a fee."

Her hand shook as she read the contents. "They want me to pay them for my grandmother's recipes? They can go to…" Bile rose in her throat, and she quickly sipped some water to keep herself from blurting out the expletive. Since she'd been back in Morrisville, her language had gotten much better.

Colin held up a palm. "Not to worry. It's just legal pandering. They've already backed down a little by saying they'll allow you to purchase the recipes. That means they really don't want them as much as they're maintaining."

"Yeah, but they haven't conceded anything yet," she snapped. The whole thing made her angry. How could she have been so stupid to fall for a jerk like Marco? Why couldn't she have seen the truth? Why was it always too little, too late?

"Calm down. They haven't yet, but they will." Colin exuded confidence, and she tried to focus on what he was saying. "The next demand letter I'll send will cite United States Appellate Court case law. I also put a staggering price on Marco's own breach of contract with you, including sending all copies of your bills for the canceled wedding and citing all the emotional distress. Did you know some states still consider infidelity subject to personal-injury litigation?"

"So a judge would uphold what you're asking?" That a judge would seemed a tad outrageous and unreal.

He took the letter from her and returned it to the folder. "We're nowhere close to filing in court any actual demands. We're still dancing around each other, negotiating. I'd say that after our next correspondence, Marco will receive a letter from his lawyers letting him know he's exhausting his retainer and asking for additional fees. At that point, he'll have to do some thinking about how much this will cost him, both monetarily and socially. I have some friends who work for the New York tabloids who owe me a favor. Cheating Italian business owners who are minor celebrities are juicy topics, especially when the fiancée found the philanderer in bed."

"I don't want to be in the papers," Rachel protested. The situation was awful enough as is. "I don't like notoriety. Neither does Marco. That was one of his biggest reasons for our staying together. He kept stating he has an image to maintain."

Colin shrugged. "Which is why we exploit that weakness. As long as he believes we will carry through on our end, we're already ahead. As it is, his lawyers and I will be having some very interesting conference calls over the next several weeks. Remember, my goal is to get your recipes declared yours, your noncompete contract invalidated and a few dollars into your hands for your hardship."

"I don't want any money," Rachel declared. "Getting the first two is more than enough. Two out of three isn't bad."

"No, but we're going for the hat trick," Colin replied, using the term for when a player scored three goals in one hockey game.

Rachel winced. "This is giving me a headache, or perhaps it's the wine I had earlier. Remind me to take your sister wine shopping before I go back to New York. I think I drank stuff out of a box. I was trying not to be snobby, but *eeuw*. There are plenty of reasonably cheap vintages that still have great taste."

He rose to his feet. "Your poor taste buds. I understand, it's like having house Scotch. Let me get you some acetaminophen for your headache. I've got some in the kitchen." He brought her two extra-strength tablets. "Take these."

"Yes, dear." She sighed, letting him know she thought the whole caretaking thing overkill.

"Have I been wrong yet?" he asked, sitting beside her and relocating the file folder to the coffee table.

She closed her eyes for a moment. "I'm sure you have. I just can't think of a time right now with my head pounding. Give me a second, though, and I'm sure one will come to mind."

"You need to let go and destress."

"Heather said that," Rachel admitted, reopening her eyes. When had he moved closer?

"That proves my point. She and I both can't be wrong." He shifted so he could put both hands on her shoulders. "You're far too tense. I can hear the knots in your back crying for relief." He then began to knead slowly, massaging her shoulders and moving his fingers to her neck. "See, you like that."

"Uh-huh," Rachel mumbled, her concentration more on his movements than on his words. His fingers were nothing short of magical. On occasion she'd gone to a masseuse at a spa in Manhattan, but her budget didn't permit the luxury often.

"Relax," he told her. "Stop thinking."

"I'm not," she lied, allowing her head to fall forward so that her chin touched her chest. She could feel the tension ebbing from her. "Where did you learn this?"

"So much for not thinking. I have no idea. Just have good fingers, I guess," Colin said, continuing to work his magic.

"I like your fingers," she replied as he rubbed out a sore spot.

"And I like you," he told her, dropping a light kiss on her nape.

The feel of his lips had her leaping forward, so that she banged her knee on the table in front of her. The water glasses wobbled. Colin grabbed for them, set them straight and moved the file folder out of harm's way, while Rachel massaged her knee.

"I'm starting to believe you've become a klutz. First my plane, now my table," he attempted to joke.

"You startled me," she defended herself. When she'd jerked away, she'd overstretched a back muscle. She rubbed it.

"Let me do that," he told her.

She scooted away. "No. You touching me will lead to nothing but trouble."

"*You* are trouble. With a capital *T.* I didn't bring you here to seduce you. Your virtue is safe," he told her.

She blinked. "I…"

"Shush. Let me finish. Please. I want to spend time with you. I like you, Rachel. You have me in knots and there's no one to massage them away but you. Hang out with me. We'll go slow."

The man could make a convincing argument. "Why do I feel as if I have no choice in the matter?" she asked resignedly.

He frowned. "You always have a choice. I'm not Marco. I won't try to make you something you're not. I believe I know you better than anyone. Deep down, you haven't changed. You're still that fearless girl who has a hidden insecure side."

"I only let *you* see that. No one else," she confessed.

He moved over, the arm of the sofa blocking her escape. "And you only let me until high school. But I know that part of you is still in there. I can sense it. You haven't hidden it as well as you think."

She sighed. "You have an annoying way of exposing my secrets."

His gaze intensified. "I'm not exposing them for all to view. And to be fair, I'll gladly share every single one of mine. The biggest is that for the first time in my life, I may not get what I want and I'm finding myself unsettled by the prospect of losing out."

She knew what—rather, who—he meant. "Me."

"You," he confirmed.

"Because I'm leaving." That fact was becoming more and more disturbing.

He slid his hand under her hair and began to massage her nape. "I care a great deal about you, and to hell with worrying about crossing a line with our lawyer-client relationship. This is way beyond that. But I can't fight you or your dream. I'm walking into any liaison with my eyes open. I know you're not planning on staying, no matter how much I wish otherwise."

She had to make him understand. "You said this situation with me was like being on a sinking ship. Well, in that case, I'm just as doomed as you. I can't fight this feeling, either, whatever this thing between us is. It almost has a life of its own. I'm scared that when I go to New York, a part of me will be left behind."

"I'll take care of whatever it is," he reassured her.

"I believe you will." A small tear escaped an eye and he used his free hand to wipe it away.

"Don't cry. This—us—will be nothing but good. I promise."

"It will be—that is, until the ride ends," she said, bringing back his words from... Had it been days ago? Weeks? She couldn't remember anymore, but at this juncture words didn't matter. Only the heart did, and she could no longer deny what hers desired.

"Until then," he agreed as he drew her into his arms and pulled her close. He kissed the top of her head, rubbing his cheek into her hair. He made no attempt to do anything but provide comfort.

About ten minutes later, Rachel lifted her head, bringing her lips to his. "I'm not ready to explore the rest of your house, but I want you to kiss me before I have to leave."

He obliged for a good long time, before finally he drew back and asked, "Will I see you tomorrow?"

"If you're brave enough to help bake," she said, nuzzling his mouth and attempting to get him to kiss her again.

"Something tells me I should stay out of that fray," he said, nipping her lips.

"Probably a wise choice. My grandmother and my mom are both planning to help, and I can probably rope Heather into assisting, as well. You'd only be in the way. We've already sifted the flour."

"So now I'm useless?" he teased.

"You're being useless. Kiss me," she demanded, turning so that she could press him back against the couch. "I say yes to a relationship with you and you deny me."

"We're dating?" he asked.

"I don't care what you call it as long as Morrisville

doesn't try to marry us off. Just keep our relationship on the down low," she said, planting another kiss on him. "Oh, I'm about to get up and leave if you don't give me incentive to stay for a little while longer."

"Then we'll negotiate our dating terms later. I'm a lawyer, remember? We like our contracts up front."

"Contract this," she said, and this time when she kissed him, Colin gave himself to her. She possessed him, and then the line between who was doing what to whom blurred.

She pulled back much later, before they did more than explore each other's mouths. "I need to go," she breathed, her chest heaving.

"If you must," he told her, not yet releasing his hold.

Regret conflicted with determination to make the correct choice. "I must. I'd like this, but part of me isn't ready for more. Not tonight. Soon. We don't have to hurry, do we?"

It was important to her that they have more time, that whatever was happening between them wasn't rushed into a few frantic, fleeting nights of bliss.

"We have time," Colin replied as she climbed out of his lap. She gathered up her things, and once he'd composed herself, he stood.

"I'm going to hate closing that door behind you. I don't think I've ever felt like this," he said.

Neither had she, and his words thrilled yet petrified her. "Try to get some sleep," she told him as she edged toward the front door.

"Only if you do the same. I don't want you to get sick again. We'll talk soon."

"I guess we can't flash code to each other anymore. I could text you," she offered as the awkwardness of a goodbye intensified.

"Relax," he said. "I'm not going anywhere. Go get some sleep. You have cakes to make."

"I'll see you before Sunday, I'm sure."

His tone had never been more serious. "Count on it."

HE'D WALKED HER OUT, kissed her again, then stood in his front doorway until the taillights of her car disappeared from view. He still couldn't believe it. She'd agreed to date him. Not even winning his first jury trial had been this elating.

Colin closed the front door and immediately sobered.

Not that this was a victory. To say that sounded mercenary. Then again, perhaps that was how he needed to approach winning over Rachel. He cared for her deeply, always had.

He hoped they'd work out the long-distance issue. But even though he feared their relationship might be over before anything began, he decided not to back down. He'd lost her in high school, and he'd been around the block enough to know he wasn't deluding himself when he said he believed she was the woman for him, for eternity.

That prospect should frighten him, but somehow it didn't. That he knew his heart reassured him even more. As for convincing her, well, he was a fighter. He meant everything he'd told her. When she left… No, he'd worry about that later. Besides, he believed in that old saying, Better to have loved and lost than never to have loved at all. In Rachel's case, though, Colin didn't plan to lose.

Chapter Ten

Rachel's phone rang Saturday at two. She answered her cell, recognizing with delight the number that popped up. "Glynnis! What's up?"

"Checking on you, that's what," Glynnis replied. "How's small-town life?"

"Not as bad as I thought," Rachel admitted. She was in the diner's kitchen, boxing up the last of the cakes. Already most of the orders had been picked up and she juggled her cell phone against her ear as she taped the box.

"Well, I heard of an interesting opportunity and wanted to pass it along your way. You know Bitsy's Bakery?"

"Yeah, that landmark place in Times Square?"

"That's the one. Well, they're searching for a chef. They want to expand into Internet orders and ship everywhere in the continental United States."

"Really?" Bitsy's Bakery had evolved into quite the destination. With more patrons than a crowded Starbucks, Bitsy's opened at 5:00 a.m., closed at 10:00 p.m. and baked twenty-four hours a day to meet both sitdown and carryout demand.

"That's what I heard and I got it straight from someone who works there. I thought it might be perfect for you."

"I want to own my own bakery," Rachel said. Then again, maybe this could be the next best thing. "Would Bitsy's let that person do some recipe development?"

"I don't know. I could ask and get back to you."

Rachel shook her head and moved the cake to the side. "It's not possible, anyway. I'm still under my noncompete with Alessandro's. My lawyer is still talking to Marco's lawyers."

"Marco is dating already," Glynnis blurted out.

"Really?" For a moment Rachel felt as though she'd been stabbed. Then, the sensation faded. She realized she simply didn't care about her ex or his new life. She'd moved on. She'd found Colin and had feelings for him, real ones that were deeper than those she'd ever shared with Marco.

"I hope he finally finds what he's looking for," Rachel said. "Maybe he'll come to his senses and be reasonable."

"Oh, I've got to go. Break's over. Keep in touch and don't be a stranger."

"I promise I won't," Rachel said. She closed her phone at the same moment Kim stuck her head in the kitchen.

"Is that ready?" she asked. "Katherine Kennedy's here."

"It is," Rachel replied, and putting Bitsy's and the future out of her head, she concentrated on today.

RACHEL'S COCONUT CAKE was a big hit at Easter brunch. She'd made two of them, one a traditional, multiple-layer cake and the other shaped like a rabbit and decorated with paper ears, licorice whiskers and jelly bean eyes. She'd put the rabbit cake on a silver tray and surrounded the cake with green-colored shredded coconut for grass, then placed jelly bean eggs all around. The kids had loved it.

The day had gone much better than Colin had expected. Although he'd only seen Rachel briefly when popping into the diner during the week, he'd given her space during the brunch. He hadn't wanted to crowd her.

The thought struck him that long ago, in high school, he'd have been full of resentment that Rachel wasn't paying attention to him. Now he knew the art of trust and patience. She'd committed to dating him, and she wasn't leaving Morrisville yet. He had time.

"So, did you get some cake?" Colin asked Bruce as both men made their way out of the dining room, past the remnants of the buffet brunch. The Morris house was full from third floor to basement, with the majority of men congregating in the family room, as was tradition.

"I did," Bruce said, taking a seat in an overstuffed recliner and kicking up his feet. "Great stuff. I had two helpings."

Colin figured now was as good as ever to reveal his news. "I heard back from Marco's lawyers. Friday. Didn't expect to get a response so soon, but they must have wanted the file off their desks for the holiday weekend."

Bruce lifted a coffee mug to his lips. "Probably realized Marco's not going to pay them anything for the issue beyond his retainer. There's no contract aside from the noncompete agreement Rachel signed when they hired her. The situation is similar to when a hairstylist moves to another salon, only in this situation, Rachel really doesn't have any clients who would follow to another restaurant," Bruce said.

"Alessandro's did sell their desserts to other establishments," Colin pointed out.

"Yes, but neither that nor her output was mentioned in her contract. This case has a lot of gray areas. Sorting them out will be like handling a divorce with no prenup. Legal fees will get very expensive on their part to prove that her recipes were works for hire."

Colin agreed. "I believe Marco's bullying her, acting in the heat of the moment. I agree that he's not going to want to pay much more."

Bruce nodded. "Probably not. It's amazing how the trivial legal issues go away when a bill's presented. You have to really want to fight for something. Legal fees aren't cheap. So what do you plan to do?"

"I picked up the phone Friday afternoon and, amazingly, got a hold of one of the attorneys handling Marco's affairs. I'm flying up to New York next Tuesday, April first, for a meeting. How's that for irony? April Fool's Day I'll fly my new plane and use the flight to acclimate to my aircraft. The plane manufacturer is buying the gas as part of our purchase contract. I got a kick out of the fact that Marco's lawyers seemed surprised I would come to them."

Bruce chuckled. "They don't know you have your own plane. They're calculating the cost, adding up the billable hours."

Colin grinned. "Yep. I figured this would give them an impression of how serious Rachel is about pursuing this. Let Marco stew a bit that she really has found the money to fight him."

"Have you told Rachel about your meeting?"

Colin shook his head. His blond hair was getting long. He'd get it trimmed before his trip to New York. "No. Not yet. I don't want her hopes up if nothing happens at the meeting. This could all be for show and for naught. We could simply be like a bunch of peacocks strutting our stuff."

"Well, good luck."

"Yeah," Colin said as Rachel entered the room. He hadn't been by her side, but they'd made plans to go to his place for movie night after the brunch ended. They left a short while later.

"So when shall we see each other again?" he asked as he kissed her goodbye long after the last movie ended. "I don't want to crowd you, but I'd like to see you often."

She placed her hand gently on the side of his face. "You're not crowding me. You're being perfect." She sighed.

"What's wrong?"

"Oh, I heard of a job opportunity yesterday. I'm a little bummed out about it." She filled him in about Bitsy's.

"We should hear something soon," Colin promised.

"You think?" She gazed at him, her eyes so full of hope.

"Yeah," he promised. "I'm in contact with them. Nothing's new, but the moment I know something you'll know."

"Thank you," she said.

Colin drew her into his arms and held her close, inhaling the floral scent of her hair. It would kill him to let her go, and as she kissed him, he let himself savor the sweetness of her lips. Then she was gone, out into the night, driving back to her house.

Fate had to be laughing at him, Colin decided. Maybe this was payback for all those women he'd dated. He'd wanted Rachel to stay. But some things couldn't be caged, and Rachel was one of them. If he loved her—and he did— he'd set her free when the time came.

SHE CALLED HIM on Tuesday, leaving him a message not to make plans and saying she was coming over. They saw each other Thursday, as well. This time he made spaghetti, the one dish he could do with ease. She'd loved it, and so had Colin. He fell more and more in love with her daily. Part of him dreaded the weekend and his meeting the following

Tuesday. If he got what he wanted from Alessandro's lawyers, for sure Rachel would leave him. As they snuggled and watched a movie, Colin wasn't ready for that.

Sunday arrived. He'd bought a bottle of wine, which was chilling in the refrigerator. He surveyed the great room as he waited for Rachel. No one would ever confuse him with Suzy Homemaker. Still, his attempt would have to do.

He could hear her car turning into his driveway, and he met her at the front door. He opened it before she could ring the bell.

"Hi," she said.

Could she be more beautiful? He could picture her arriving home like this every day, and deep in his heart he knew he'd never tire of her. If only she wasn't so determined to return to New York.

"Hey."

He stepped out of the way and reached for her coat, which she was taking off.

She smiled and he was lost. "So did you just miss me?"

She would never realize how much. He'd played golf with his father this afternoon while Rachel had cooked. But his thoughts had been on her all day.

Before he could answer, she withdrew a small two-inch box from her purse. "I brought you a treat. I made snickerdoodles and I have three cookies in here for you."

She was already removing the treats, and he groaned. "You know snickerdoodles are my favorite."

Her eyes darkened as she waved one under his nose so he could inhale the cinnamon scent. "Mmm-hmm. I remembered from high school. I didn't forget what you liked. You used to try everything I cooked, even the stuff that didn't look very appetizing."

"It was all delicious."

"Liar," she teased, lifting one of the bite-size morsels to his lips. Colin couldn't resist, and he wrapped his mouth around her fingertips and sucked hard, drawing in the cookie. The pastry melted on his tongue, the sweet cinnamon creating a delicious aftertaste. He immediately wanted more.

"You closed your eyes. They're that good?" Rachel asked.

"Didn't you sample them?"

"I had a few earlier," she admitted.

Colin hauled her to him and pressed her close. "So you should know the answer." Then he brought his mouth down to hers.

"Good, aren't they?" he asked between kisses.

"Oh, yes," she replied, running her fingers into his hair. "Kiss me again."

"I thought we were going to eat," he said. "I've got steaks ready to barbecue and—"

"I'm feasting," Rachel replied. He drew back so he could gaze into her brown eyes. "No. Don't stop," she breathed. "Not now."

She was pure temptation. He'd waited forever, and despite himself could wait a little more. "I need to tell you something," Colin began. He couldn't let either of them begin making love without him explaining about his trip to New York or how he felt about her.

She tugged at his shirt, getting it loose. Her hands were immediately on his chest. "Whatever it is, it can wait. I can't."

"It really can't…" he protested, stepping back, the lawyer in him wanting to do the right thing.

"It can," she insisted, moving closer and sliding her fingers down to his belly button.

"If you're sure," Colin said, ready to lose this particular battle when she'd removed her hands from his chest, took his fingertip and traced it over her lips. Then she drew the end of his finger to her mouth. Colin groaned and succumbed.

He pulled his hand free and replaced it with his mouth. He sucked her tongue and his lower body quickened. Realizing his eyes were closed, he opened them. He slid his hands underneath Rachel's sweater and found the lacy texture of her bra. He could deny himself no longer. He kissed her neck, the skin revealed at the V-neckline, and then he simply yanked the shirt up and kissed her through the lace.

She wore pink. Somehow he'd known that she really was a girlie girl, given to feminine tastes. She kept up such a tough exterior, but beneath hid someone fragile. He would never hurt her as others had.

He scooped her up and carried her into his bedroom. He set her on the bed, losing himself as his teeth nibbled, his mouth suckled and her body went wild.

"That's right, let go," he whispered as he moved his kisses to her other breast. Then with deft fingers he began undoing the buttons of her jeans. He wanted her wearing nothing but her skin, so he moved himself between her legs and slid the denim material down. He felt her inner thigh clench as he placed a wet kiss there, and then he simply placed his whole mouth over the pink lace she wore and kissed her through.

As HER CLIMAX began, Rachel turned her head to the left. She could think of nothing but what Colin was doing to her, and the pleasure he'd cajoled out of her very willing body.

She fisted the bedsheet in a weak attempt to get a grip,

but found herself denied as Colin's lips bit the pink material of her lace panties and tugged them down. She then was naked, her green polished toes the subject of his interrogation as he tickled the soles of her feet. "Cute," he said before sliding forward to bring his head back to taste her sweetness one more time.

She opened her eyes, and saw Colin concentrating on nothing but her pleasure. The intensity of this man overwhelmed her. As he brought her to orgasm again, she let her head fall back onto the pillow and forgot her worries.

She'd ached for Colin for far too long. He was making love to her because he wanted *her,* no one else. She'd fallen in love with him. If nothing else, this past week had cemented those feelings. Rachel couldn't deny herself this night, even if it caused her heartbreak later. The future could take care of itself. She'd think about it tomorrow.

He brought his face next to hers and kissed her lips, and it was then she realized he had way too many clothes on. She ran her hands underneath his clothing, touching his chest everywhere. She tugged at his shirt, and, as if sensing her intentions, Colin broke their kiss, pulled off the offending apparel and threw it aside.

"Do you know how much I want you?" he whispered. She arched her back and he moved his mouth down her body one last time before resting over her on all fours. She reached for the buttons of his pants and made him take everything off. Her fingers found him, and he groaned as she continued her caress.

"Look at me," he said, escaping her touch.

Her gaze connected with his. He leaned over her, face close, blue eyes intense. Not one part of his body touched hers and she desired that contact.

Colin gave her lips a quick kiss. "This is real for me. I care about you, more than you know. Once we do this, it changes everything. Are you positive you want this? That you're ready?"

Was she? Rachel blinked. She'd been certain the moment she'd gotten in her car and driven over here.

He leaned closer, still not touching. "I might have a little caveman in me, because I'm feeling damn possessive about you. When I enter you, you're mine."

Maybe it was the way his eyes seemed to twinkle or the way his eyes crinkled that took the edge off how serious his words were. Maybe it was just her overwhelming need to make her lifelong fantasy a reality.

Whatever it was, she needed Colin as much as she needed to breathe. She trusted him, treasured him deeply. "Yes. I'm sure," she said.

Tears formed as the enormity of the moment struck her. They were joined. Colin was her other half. He had made her whole.

"YOU OKAY?" Colin asked her about ten minutes later. After each had used the restroom, they'd crawled back onto the bed and simply held each other without speaking. Rachel was afraid words might cloud things. Already her mind and heart conflicted.

They'd finally made love and it had been everything she'd ever dreamed and more.

Her decision to give herself to him hadn't been easy. She still planned on returning to New York. Colin was like chocolate. Ask any woman and it would be the last thing she could give up if she had to diet. So how could Rachel walk away from the best man she'd ever met, who'd just given her the best lovemaking of her life, whom she'd loved since childhood?

That was why, although she'd agreed to date him, she'd wrestled with her choice over the weekend. In the final analysis, she'd realized that she was like a tumbleweed, caught up in the whirlwind that he was to her, and unable to control her destiny when it came to him.

Being with Colin, in the most fundamental way possible, was simply ordained, maybe from the day she'd been brought home to the house next door, where an eighteen-month-old Colin toddled around in diapers.

She'd seen his childhood bedroom, but this adult room reflected the man he'd become. The furnishings were sparse, just a king-size bed, a nightstand and a chest of drawers. He had miniblinds, no curtains of any kind on the two windows flanking the bed. Overhead, a ceiling fan circled lazily in the vaulted ceiling, pushing the warm air down on their cooling bodies. All the room required was a woman's touch.

And yet, despite her strongest feelings for him, she couldn't be that woman.

Chapter Eleven

Colin couldn't believe it. By the time he left New York City around 2:00 Tuesday afternoon, he had the entire outcome he'd hoped for, including a check for two thousand dollars to cover Marco's portion of the nonrefundable deposits. Colin had scored the hat trick.

The win was bittersweet. He'd scored a great victory, proving his merit as a legal mind. However, at the same time, Rachel was free. Free to go back to New York and work, free to start her own business, free to keep her recipes. Marco hadn't even bothered to appear at the law office, letting his attorneys decide everything. Word from Colin's tabloid-reporter contact was that Marco Alessandro had already found someone new and simply wanted to put this "mess" behind him.

Since Alessandro's didn't open until five and that was still a few hours away, Colin had flown home instead of going over to the restaurant and punching the man in the nose for declaring Rachel a mess he simply had to "mop up."

"So you like it?" the company representative in the copilot's seat said, interrupting Colin's thoughts.

"Love it," Colin replied. The Cessna 182 he and his

friends had bought was everything they'd hoped for. For years they had flown a variety of planes and finally settled on this one. Of course, he'd had to beg to fly the plane first, but his friends had capitulated once Colin had agreed to pay for everyone's round of golf at the next course they flew to play at. He had no doubt they'd hit him up for somewhere expensive, like Pebble Beach. He really didn't mind.

The day was clear and sunny, perhaps a good omen that maybe Rachel wouldn't flee so fast. They'd been together all last week, spent the entire weekend together. He smiled to himself, thinking how lucky he was. She'd been insatiable last night, not that he minded. He called Rachel, got her voice mail, told her he had news and that he'd try her again but to meet him at eight at his place.

His phone rang as he was getting into his car after parking the plane in its hangar. "So what's going on?" Rachel asked.

"I have news," he told her when she answered.

"Okay? So what is it? Is it about this past weekend? Or last night? Wait, for a minute I forgot. You went flying today. You love your new plane," she said.

"Well, that's part of it," Colin hedged. He'd decided to keep the secret that he had a meeting with Marco's lawyers from her. He'd wanted to tell her but hadn't been able to. He didn't want the best relationship or lovemaking of his life tainted by thoughts of her leaving him.

"There's more?" Rachel asked.

He adjusted his earpiece. "Yes. I have a surprise for you."

"Ooh. Does it involve candles? I got invited to a candle party on Thursday night. Since the last home party wasn't bad, I'm going. I can buy you something for your bland, beige house then."

He chuckled. "I can make tonight involve candles. But then you better meet me at eight-thirty so I can prepare."

"No, eight's fine. Candlelight's overrated. And do you mind if we order pizza? Now that Easter's over, my mom's been on a salad kick. There's nothing good to eat."

Colin laughed. That was his earthy Rachel.

He said goodbye and disconnected, then drove to the quick mart located inside a gas station at the Highway 74 overpass. By the time he got home, took a quick shower and changed into more casual clothes, he had only ten minutes before Rachel arrived.

However, she didn't want pizza or his news. The minute she stepped in the door and kissed him, passion ruled.

"So WILL IT always be like this?" she asked him afterward, overwhelmed by how he made her feel. With him she was not only well sexed, but she was cherished. Loved, although he hadn't yet spoken the word to her.

"I hope so," he said, tracing a finger along her jaw. "I meant what I told you the first time we made love."

She stared at the ceiling, watching the wooden fan circle around as she tried to remember. "About what?"

"You being mine. Not that I own you or anything. But Rachel, you're it for me. I don't think anyone could ever follow you."

That could simply not be possible. "You're giving me too much credit," she protested.

He leaned on an elbow, edging closer. "No, you're not giving yourself enough credit. You've stolen my heart. I knew you would going into this, and I'm prepared. Or so I thought until..." His words drifted off.

"Lovemaking does change everything, doesn't it? And

then it changes nothing," Rachel said with a sigh, depressed. She loved him, yet her city beckoned. "At some point, I'm going to have to walk away from you and go home." She paused as a hopeful thought took hold. "You could come with me."

"To New York?"

"Yes." While making the offer surprised her, the idea held appeal. "I'm sure they need attorneys there."

He shook his head, dashing the possibility. "I've thought about it, believe me. I even made a pro-con list last week. I'm up for partner this year. I don't want to be a faceless attorney in one of those supersize firms that concentrate only on billable hours. I like being in a small town, where everyone knows everyone else and actually cares about your well-being. Lancaster and Morris is my father's legacy and my destiny. Once I stopped running and accepted who I am, I was content with my future, and ready to embrace it."

"Morrisville is so stifling," she argued, a tad angry at his rejection.

"Not when you have a plane. It's just a jumping-off point. Chris—" he named one of his plane partners "—is taking his wife to Maui for a week. He plans to fly over the islands, take pictures of the volcano vents and lava flows that other tourists don't get to see."

That sounded absolutely wonderful and she focused on that to calm her tumultuous feelings. "I've never been to Hawaii."

"Neither have I. Let's go," he proposed.

She stared at him. He was serious, and the invitation so tempting. But life wasn't that simple or easy, at least not in her experience. She exhaled slowly, accepting the sad truth.

"You'd hate New York City," she stated, getting back to the matter at hand.

He nodded. "Living there, yes. But I think it's a great place to visit. You might even get me to one of those Broadway shows once in a while. I've heard many of them are quite good."

"Would you do it for me?"

She meant live there, and he understood, because he shook his head and said, "We'd hate each other."

Rachel closed her eyes, savoring the bittersweet irony. He'd move to New York and be with her. But he wouldn't be happy. She couldn't relocate Colin.

"I know. You'd resent it there," she said quietly, accepting the truth.

"I'd try not to," he replied. "But it's not right for me. We'd suffer. Maybe fight. I think that would be worse. If…"

She put a finger to her lips, silencing him. He'd give her the world if he could, but this was not something he could do. She slowly shook her head as sadness consumed her.

"You're right. It won't work. It's like caging a wild animal. Animals need their habitats. You're one who can't be transplanted. You thrive here."

"I do. I also believe you will, as well. You could move back here permanently if you really wanted to. Like you did those home parties, I think you'd discover life isn't so bad. You stopped running away long ago. Admit it, Rachel, being home this time wasn't water torture. Was probably even better than you hoped. You believe a big city is what's necessary to launch your bakery. But you can do that here. You've been happy since you returned."

No, living in New York made her happy. But it hadn't

made her content. There was a huge difference between the two. Contentment lasted. Happiness could be fleeting. For the first time, she hesitated. Could her future really be here? In Morrisville with Colin? Rachel's stomach growled, saving her from a reply. "Oops."

"Let's order that pizza," Colin said. "Domino's in Batesville delivers here. What do you want?"

"Everything," she said, referring to more than just pizza toppings.

About forty minutes later, she and Colin had both dressed and were sitting on his great-room sofa, eating a large thin-crust deluxe.

"So you said you had news," she said, flipping off the television. Now that she and Colin were dressed, she wasn't interested in the nightly news, but in what Colin had to tell her.

"I did. I took out the new plane today."

She reached for another slice. "I can't wait for you to take me up. I've been hearing all about this Blue Owl Bakery in Kimmswick, Missouri, and I want to check it out. It sounds like something that might work for me."

"So now you're using me," he said, washing down a bite with a drink of cola.

She wiped a crumb from the corner of his lips. He was adorable. Already she anticipated kissing him, after she'd had nourishment for the upcoming activity she intended to indulge in again. "I'll make it worth your while. Now, what is this big secret you keep refusing to reveal?"

"My flight location." He stuffed another bite in his mouth, and as he chewed, Rachel found herself suddenly frustrated. He'd mentioned seeing her. So what was with making her ask Twenty Questions?

"Okay, next?" she prodded.

His expression turned serious. "I flew up for a meeting with Marco's lawyers. I also spoke with my friend at the tabloid newspaper."

"So what happened?" She returned the remaining part of the pizza slice to her plate. No wonder Colin had been so hesitant. Habit had her prepared for the worst.

Colin covered her hand gently with his. "Marco's moved on. He's found someone new. Declared himself in love."

"I know—Glynnis told me. It didn't take long," Rachel said scathingly. She snatched her hand away. "The bastard never could keep his pants zipped. I told him this was how everything would go down, but did he listen to me? No, of course not. He had to make some silly power play and try to take my recipes. He didn't get my recipes, did he?"

Colin shook his head. "No. In fact, he backed down on that. In my briefcase, which is in my office here, I have a signed, notarized statement from Marco, as agent of Alessandro's, giving up all rights to your recipes and releasing you from your noncompete contract. I also have a check payable to you for two thousand dollars."

Her mouth dropped. This couldn't be happening, but it was. "You're kidding. No, I can see you're not. This means…"

"You're free," Colin said simply.

"Oh, my God! We won! You did it!" She was elated. "I don't owe him anything?"

His guarded expression never changed. He had no elation. No joy. "No. It's over. His lawyers suggested you avoid Alessandro's and Marco."

"I don't care about either. And money! You got the hat trick!"

"I did."

This was the best news. Excitement consumed her. She'd won! "So I have enough to get back on my feet. I have a little saved up. Those Easter cakes really helped and you just got me more."

She tossed her arms around him; luckily, Colin had already moved his plate, or the pizza would have gone flying. "I can't believe you did it! I mean, of course I knew you could. Thank you! Thank you so much."

He nodded. "I have a bottle of champagne to celebrate, but we sort of got sidetracked when you arrived...."

Rachel then realized Colin wasn't thrilled by all this great news. She'd expected to have everything drag out. That she'd be stuck in Morrisville until August. It was early April, and she was free to go back to New York anytime. She could be back in the city by her birthday. She could leave tomorrow if she so chose.

Elation turned to remorse as she became conscious of the implications and his somber demeanor. When he'd made love to her tonight, he'd known what she would do. He'd known the moment he told her his news that she'd want to go back to New York.

He loved her.

He didn't have to say the words, but her heart recognized the truth. "Oh, my God, I'm so sorry," she said.

"Just waiting until you figured it out," he said calmly. "Forgive me if I'm not as wild about you winning this case as you. I prepared for this, but it's still hard. You need to do what's best for you. I support you in everything. You know that."

She struggled to maintain her composure. Her body still ached from his lovemaking, but she couldn't stay in Morrisville. He'd given her back her wings. She had to fly and she could only do that in New York. She pressed his hand to her heart. "I'll always have you here. I'm…" Tears threatened and Rachel stood. How ironic that she was running away again.

"Will I see you before you leave?" he asked.

She'd never felt such an immediate urgency to escape. "No. I'd rather slip out like a thief in the night. I don't want Morrisville throwing me some bon voyage party." And if she saw him again, she'd be torn. She might not be able to make her feet move. Her dream or Colin. When had the choice become that hard? Probably the moment she'd fallen in love with him.

"I guess Heather and Kristin will have to cancel the party they were planning."

So they had been thinking of something for her thirtieth birthday. She'd suspected a secret. Her guilt intensified. "Well, you know me—I'm not the party type. But I'll be back to visit. I won't be a stranger."

Yet she already was, and this truth seeped into her bones, where it became mired in the pain overwhelming her. All these people cared for her. They'd understand, but her leaving would hurt them. Never had she been this conflicted. The door to her future had opened and she hesitated about going through.

"I'll walk you out."

She rose to her feet and wobbled. "No. I couldn't bear it. Just stay here and finish your pizza. I know the way."

"That I don't doubt," Colin said.

His tone was harsh, bitter, and she fled. If he'd followed her or touched her, she might not have the strength to do what had to be done. She might not have been able to leave.

When she entered her silent childhood home a half hour later, she realized she'd have to break the news to her grandmother and mother, who weren't going to be happy, either. Still, Rachel could be back in New York by the weekend. Nothing seemed "right" anymore, though she was free to follow her dream. As the world around her seemed to implode, she focused on that.

COLIN SAT THERE long after the pizza had grown cold. He finally stood and threw the remains in the trash. He'd had to set her free. He couldn't have done the long-distance thing, and he couldn't live in New York any more than she could live in Morrisville. They loved each other, but they loved their own cities more. The realization stung, yet he'd known this was going to happen. Still, one was never prepared for the ensuing pain.

He remembered that old saying his mother would use—that if you loved something, you had to set it free. And that if it came back to you, it was yours. If not, the love wasn't meant to be.

He loved Rachel. He had set her free. He didn't delude himself, though. She wouldn't be coming back.

Chapter Twelve

"Rachel, we need those cookies out there stat! All that's left on the tray in the case are crumbs. These cookies don't have to be perfect, just iced. Chop, chop! Time is money!"

"Coming right up," Rachel said. She wiped the back of her hand over her brow, not because she was sweating but because she was stressed. She'd been working at Bitsy's Bakery for almost a week. Today was her thirtieth birthday, and here she was—at 11:15 a.m. on April 15, the deadline for people to file their United States taxes—piping the last drops of decorative blue frosting onto a few dozen of Bitsy's world-famous butterfly-shaped cookies.

As discontent settled, Rachel reminded herself that she was lucky to have gotten the decent-paying job. She'd also scored the weekday shift, starting at nine-thirty and ending at six. She'd arrived back in New York too late to get the job as Bitsy's Internet-development person. However, the restaurant manager who'd hired her had promised Rachel lots of connections, and she hadn't had to sign a noncompete agreement. So there was a silver lining in the melancholy Rachel was experiencing.

She hadn't expected to be so busy, but at least that kept the loneliness at bay. She'd been running on adrenaline since her return to Manhattan. Sadly, this time when she crashed, Colin wouldn't be there to reheat broccoli-cheese soup.

She tried to get him out of her head, but like every other time, she failed. She thought of him constantly, wondering what she was doing. She hadn't had much contact with anyone from Morrisville, including her family. They'd been very disappointed in her decision.

Her cell phone had been silent, adding to her stress. Life in New York had moved on while she'd been away; the city hadn't missed her in the slightest. Aside from Glynnis, she no longer was friends with those she'd known when she'd dated Marco. Of course, once she'd taken up with Marco, she'd lost many of the friends she'd made when she'd first arrived in the city at eighteen. At that time she'd been eager to escape Morrisville and hadn't really appreciated all she'd left behind. Now she felt a profound sense of loss, as if she'd left behind part of her soul.

She tried to think positively. She'd started out alone in the city once before, and she could do it again. She was just a year or two off on her goal plan, that was all. It happened, and she'd deal.

"Rachel! Cookies! Now," Bertha Blevins, Rachel's supervisor, yelled again. Bitsy, the restaurant's namesake, had retired long ago to Long Island and let the management company she'd hired run the business. Bertha supervised the day shift.

Rachel thought the woman fit the negative connotation of her name perfectly. Not wanting to incur Bertha's wrath any more than was necessary, Rachel finished the cookies and toted them out to where the constant crowd waited.

"SO HAVE YOU heard from Rachel?" Reginald asked Kim. He was seated at the diner counter. It wasn't Reginald's regular spot—he preferred the booth in the corner—but he'd chosen the seat because of its proximity to Kim.

He glanced at Harold, who was seated next to him, reading the editorial section of the local newspaper. Hmm, Reginald thought. Maybe the old guy had a method to his madness. He'd probably had a thing for Kim for years. She'd been single about as long as Harold had. Reginald realized he might have solved one of Morrisville's mysteries, one Kim probably had figured out long ago.

Kim finished ringing up a customer, then grabbed a pot of coffee and refilled Reginald's cup. "I called her a few days ago to say happy birthday. She sounded fine, but I think it's a cover-up. She's not as happy as she's pretending. She's not even living in her former apartment. Because she hadn't wanted to lose the rent-controlled studio, she'd signed a contract subletting the place for the full six months of her noncompete, and the person won't be out until August. She's staying in some cheap residence hotel one step above a dump—although she didn't come right out and say that. She said staying there was helping her save money."

"She seemed all fired up to get out of here," Reginald observed.

Kim agreed. "Packed the next day and drove off." She paused and wiped her hands on her apron. "We were a bit surprised Colin got her legal issues settled so fast."

"I don't believe he was expecting such quick results," Reginald said. "Having Rachel's case finished certainly didn't help his love life. He's besotted with her, and now that she's left, he's moping. Can't stand it when that boy sulks. He's got a brand-new plane and isn't interested in anything but working. Never seen that boy so dedicated to the firm. Says he's determined not to give me any reason to not name him full partner this year. Sure, his dedication is what I want, but he's lost some of his spunk. He's on overkill trying to prove himself worthy. He'll make full partner. However, I've got quite a few years left before I turn over my part of the firm to him."

"But that's been your plan all along, right?" Kim asked, resting a hip against the counter.

Reginald nodded and added more sugar to his cup. "I made sure to clarify. Colin told me he wouldn't be happy in New York, even if he wasn't taking over the family firm. Seems he and Rachel are… What was the term he used the other day? Oh, yes, geographically challenged."

Kim topped up Harold's mug. "A shame. I'd never seen her happier than when she was baking here. She'd even started writing a business plan. When I spoke with her, I asked her how that was going, and she told me she just didn't have time."

"She'll never have time. Maybe she'll wise up sooner than later and realize it," he said.

"She's too stubborn," Kim replied, setting the coffeepot aside. "She'll never notice what's under her nose. She had everything that was important to her here."

"Maybe you should show her what she's missing," Harold said. The old codger had lowered his newspaper. Clearly, he'd been listening to every word.

"I'm not understanding you," Kim said, interested in Harold's viewpoint.

He reached for the silver cream pitcher, poured, then stirred. "I doubt anyone up there cares for her. Not like the people in this town do. Up there she's just one face in a sea of faces. Perhaps a little Morrisville needs to go to New York. Tell her that her bear claws are better than yours."

"They are?" Kim's indignation came fast.

Harold nodded and took a sip of his coffee. An undercurrent passed between him and Kim. Reginald found the exchange fascinating. "Ah. Show her our support," Kim clarified.

"Show her exactly what she's missing," Harold replied. He wiped his lips and put his napkin back on his lap to emphasize his point. "You."

RACHEL HAD SURVIVED a couple more weeks at Bitsy's Bakery. It was now the second of May, and Manhattan was starting to celebrate the nicer weather that appeared with the month's arrival. People were outside more, and flowers had begun to bloom. This was the time of year Rachel liked best—the longer days, the lifting of the spirit before the oppressive summer heat sapped everyone's energy.

Well, she wouldn't be heading to the Hamptons at any point this year, she thought wryly as she placed a tray of cookies in the oven to bake. She set the timer and gestured to her coworker. "I'm going home. You'll need to get these out in eight minutes."

"Will do."

Rachel made her way back to the staff area—basically, a wall with some high-school lockers—took off her apron and threw it in the linen hamper. Today was Friday, and thankfully, Rachel didn't have to work weekends.

She exited and began to walk south, then cut over a block to catch the subway. Her residence hotel was about four stops south of Bitsy's. Her current digs were nothing special, but at least the area was safe.

The best she could afford without digging into her financial settlement, the residence hotel rented rooms by the month. The place shoeboxed everyone in between paper-thin walls. Somehow her room fit a twin bed, love seat, table, two chairs, TV and a small kitchenette. Add one closet and a tiny bathroom barely large enough to turn around in, and Rachel had a home.

Once in the room, she set her purse down and flopped into one of the chairs. Her feet hurt. She glanced at her closed laptop. She'd opened up her business plan last night and began looking at the ideas she'd typed up for Sweet Sensations. She should be taking Mother's Day cake orders. But she didn't have a Web site, and so far she'd been too exhausted from the grind at Bitsy's to look for a kitchen to rent—not that she'd be able to afford one in the city, anyway. What had made her ever think she could? Maybe she'd been deluding herself all these years. Maybe her goal was just a pipe dream, something never to be achieved.

A knock sounded at the door. Rachel sighed. Probably the neighbor two doors down. In the spirit of making new friends, Rachel had gone to a club with her last Friday night. Rachel hadn't enjoyed herself much, but the girl had had a ball, and had taken home some guy Rachel wouldn't have touched with a ten-foot pole.

She'd been hit on, certainly, but not one man could compare with Colin Morris. She'd gone home alone.

"God, I'm doomed," Rachel muttered as she strode to the door. She peered through the peephole, and started in surprise. "No way." She unchained the door and turned the knob. "What are you doing here?"

"Is that any way to greet me? I don't fly very often, you know." Her grandmother marched in, glanced around and gave a low whistle. "Not like my room at the Millennium, that's for sure."

The surprises didn't end.

"You're here for a holiday?"

Kim nodded. "Yep. Until Monday. You can walk to most of the theaters from my hotel. I have tickets to two shows tomorrow. Now, give your grandmother a hug. Took me a while to find this place."

Rachel gasped with worry as she hugged her petite grandmother. "You didn't walk here?" The Millennium Broadway was on Forty-second Street, just east of Times Square. Bitsy's was only a block north of there.

"Oh, I rode in a cab. Crazy man didn't speak much English, but we made it. I have to admit, I held on tight. I've never seen so many cars."

"Is my mother here, too?"

Kim shook her head. "Someone had to stay and run the diner, and you know Adrienne. She's not the traveling type."

Rachel smiled as she thought of her mom. "She never has been. She's never left Indiana, so I always understood why she never considered visiting me," Rachel said.

"That woman lets the grass grow under her feet. She's never been one for any type of adventure. Now me—I figured it was high time to visit you. I've never been here before, but I'm always open to any new experience."

"I'm so glad you're here. So you just arrived today? You didn't travel alone, did you?"

"Nope. Loretta Morris came with me. We've been talking about a trip like this forever. She's been to Manhattan a few times already and she said she'd show me the ropes.

She's taking a nap, so I had some free time. We're going to walk Times Square later tonight, see all the freaky people and revel in the neon lights."

Rachel suppressed a smile at her grandmother's reference to "freaky" people. New York was simply a melting pot where you would see all sorts. "Well, come and have a seat. Do you have a minute or two?"

"I do," Kim said. She glanced around. "You're not this messy at home."

Rachel felt a pang of shame at the shabby condition of the room. "I'm not here enough and these rooms don't have maid service. I have laundry to do, and then I'll put everything away. At least the dishes are clean. The chef in me won't stand a messy work space, even if the kitchen's not much of one."

"Speaking of kitchens, Harold says hello. He wants you to know that your bear claws are better than mine. I wasn't exactly happy to hear that, mind you, although I guess it's the truth. Your coconut cake remains the talk of the town."

Perhaps that was because little happened in Morrisville, Rachel thought. Still, the compliment touched her. Morrisville expanding its provincial taste buds? Who would have thought that possible?

"Also, everyone's asking if they'll be able to order Mother's Day cakes, and if you have your Web site done and are ready for business," Kim finished.

Rachel wished. "I haven't had the time to work on anything. Even if I did, I'd still be without a kitchen. This venture is turning out to be a lot more complicated than I thought." Speaking of thoughts, one popped into her head. "Did Colin fly you here?"

"He did," her grandmother said. "Best plane ride I've ever had. Loretta and I both rode in back and talked over those headsets. We brought our own beverages. Quite comfortable. No restroom, but I'm still spry enough to hold it."

Rachel grimaced. Too much information. Her grandmother's candor was sometimes unsettling.

"So is Colin staying over in the city, as well?" Rachel asked, struggling to keep her tone casual.

Her grandmother shook her head. "No. He dropped us off at noon today, and turned around and flew home. He's flying up here Monday around one to pick us up. We have tickets to more shows on Sunday."

"Oh." Rachel had to admit she was disappointed. She'd be working and wouldn't get a chance to see him. She'd missed him. Terribly. Sure, it had been her choice to return to New York and get her life back. But she was starting to wonder how much of a life it really was.

She'd found love and walked away from it. How many nights had her fingers hovered over the keypad of her cell phone, ready to dial his number? She'd closed the device each time and tossed it aside in frustration.

"Well, I just wanted to check on how you're doing. Loretta and I have eight-thirty dinner reservations at Tavern on the Green. A little late, but the best we could get."

Rachel stood, disbelieving. This was it? The entire visit? Pop in, pop out? "Will I get to see you again?"

Kim shook her head. "Probably not. Today we went shopping and toured the Empire State Building. We have such a full schedule. We want to travel to Ellis Island in the morning and track our ancestors. We have to be up pretty early. On Sunday morning we're visiting some museum the moment it opens. Loretta knows the name."

"It was good to see you," Rachel said, disappointed that her grandmother wasn't spending more time with her.

"You don't make it home often enough, so I wanted to at least stop by and say hello while I was in your neck of the woods."

"I'm glad you stopped by," Rachel said.

"Me, too. I miss you, dear. More than you'll know," Kim said, giving Rachel another hug.

And with that, her grandmother left, and soon Rachel wondered if she'd been there at all. About a half hour later, she unlocked her door to admit the neighbor girl, who went away disappointed that Rachel wasn't up to the club circuit that night.

Rachel picked up her cell phone. Then set it back down. Then, determined, she picked it up again, flipped it open and pressed the keys for the number she knew by heart. It rang once before voice mail answered.

"Hi. You've reached Colin Morris. I'm sorry I'm not available to take your call, but if you leave your name and number after the beep, I'll return your call as soon as possible."

Longing consumed her. She'd missed hearing his voice. So where was he? She'd let him go, so she had to prepare for the worst. He was probably on a date. Maybe he just didn't want to talk to her. She closed the phone, reminding herself that she'd always made her own choices. No one had ever persuaded her to do otherwise. Her melancholy was her own darn fault.

COLIN STARED at the phone. The number that had come up on caller ID was none other than Rachel's. She hadn't left a message.

Should he call her back? Take the call as a small gesture? Would hearing her voice improve things?

Here it was, Friday night, and he was having dinner in the country club's golf-course bar—aptly named the Nineteenth Hole because this was a place where those getting off the course lingered. After parking his plane following his return trip from New York, Colin had played nine holes himself. Golf was a sport you could do alone and no one would think you a loser with no friends.

His father had been the one who'd suggested taking the four-day weekend, under the guise of getting his mother and Kim Palladia to Manhattan, of course.

Colin pushed his plate away. He'd finished and the bartender snagged the remains of his dinner. "Wrap this?"

"No," Colin said. Again, he stared at the phone number, then, with a resigned sigh, put the phone back in his pocket. He couldn't bear to talk to Rachel when the answer would've been the same. She wasn't coming back.

"RACHEL! WE NEED more chocolate chip cookies for the front display case."

Used to the refrain, Rachel dusted her hands on her apron. "On my way." She'd been about to start mixing the chocolate cake batter, but that would have to wait.

"And Rachel. As soon as you do that and get those cakes in the oven, then I need you to…" Bertha rattled off a long list. Rachel nodded her acceptance of the assignments and kept her resentment hidden. She wasn't afraid of hard work, but her current boss was a slave driver. Bertha's attitude was that all her employees should be grateful they had jobs, and that if they messed up, they could easily be replaced. Case in point—Rachel had taken the job of someone who'd been fired. She grabbed the cookies from the storage tubs and began to prepare a tray. If this were her kitchen, she'd be more organized. For the volume of business Bitsy's did, it amazed Rachel how inefficient the place was—for example, taking her away from mixing so she could load cookie trays.

Someone should know ahead of time what was needed in the front showcases, not just realize that things were empty after the last pastry was sold. Bitsy's restocked as necessary, not first thing in the morning, like Kim's.

Rachel brought the new tray out front and removed the old tray first. She noted that sugar cookies were low. And she knew that in less than half an hour she'd be forced to stop what she was doing and return to the display case again.

She carried the empty tray back to the kitchen. "I probably should have brought sugar cookies out, as well," she told Bertha.

"There are still some left, and I'll tell you when to do things. That's my job. You concentrate on yours. You're already behind."

Perhaps it was Bertha's tone. Perhaps it was that the past few weeks hadn't been what Rachel had expected of her return, but something inside her snapped. She was tired. Exhausted. Crabby. And not willing to take any more.

"I'm behind because you keep interrupting me to give me more things to do. I could have carried two trays out there. That would have saved time."

"Are you questioning me?" Bertha retorted, disbelieving.

"I'm saying you yourself could be more efficient," Rachel said tartly. She glanced at the clock. It was only eleven-fifteen. She'd worked only forty-five minutes so far. It was Monday and her shift didn't end until six. She had the rest of the day, the rest of the week, the rest of the month and the rest of the year to tolerate this—

Suddenly, life became crystal clear, as it had that moment in Alessandro's when she'd thrown the cake on Marco. The problem wasn't this kitchen, or Alessandro's or even Marco. The problem was Rachel. To misquote President Harry Truman, the buck stopped with her.

She'd been forgetting that. It wasn't a place that made you happy; it was the people who occupied that place.

She'd needed the anonymity of New York in her twenties to make mistakes, to develop her own culinary skills away from the high standard that her family set.

Kim's Diner was a destination and a home for half the town. If she'd remained in Morrisville after high school, she'd never have emerged from under her grandmother's shadow. Here in New York she'd learned to make bear claws better than her grandmother's. Harold wouldn't lie about something like that, and Kim wouldn't have repeated the statement unless it was true. Her grandmother had wonderful culinary skills. But Rachel had taken Kim's recipes and improved them.

Rachel had spent her birthday alone, no cake, no candles, no party, no presents. But she was thirty now, a grown-up. Her own woman. Her own chef. And she didn't need to let her dream die in this city where power trips could be the norm.

For the first time she realized she wouldn't run away anymore. It was time to run *to* something. She'd be entering the race late, but hopefully, she could still cross the finish line and have everything she'd ever wanted.

"I quit—" Rachel announced.

The shocked expression on Bertha's face was priceless.

She actually stammered. "Y-y-you can't quit. You're in the middle of a cake."

Rachel shrugged as the oppression and stress lifted from her shoulders and she was no longer weighed down. The moment was a revelation. "You're the supervisor. You finish it.... Oh—and mail my final paycheck. Have a great day." Rachel turned on her heel, dropped her apron in the bin and grabbed her purse.

She wasn't wanted at Bitsy's anymore, there was a place Rachel *was* wanted. Somewhere she belonged, with a man who'd loved her enough to let her go. Rachel glanced at the clock in Times Square as she headed for the subway. She'd return for her car and her belongings later in the week. Right now, she needed to hurry. She had a plane to catch. She was flying home.

TRUST HIS MOTHER and Kim to be late, Colin thought as he stood outside his plane. Not that they would be going anywhere soon. He was flying under visual flight rules, and the early-afternoon storm forming meant takeoff would be delayed.

He glanced at his watch. One-forty. Forty minutes behind schedule and about to be a lot more. No use worrying about takeoff now.

He let his irritation go, calming himself. His mother and Kim weren't to blame. He'd seen for himself on his visit to Marco's attorneys the horrors of New York City traffic. Plus today was a Monday, it was lunchtime and there were more than a few road-construction projects on the Jersey Turnpike. He could be waiting for quite a while.

He just itched to get back in the air. He made one more circle around the Cessna 182. He had to admit he loved his plane— His phone buzzed, and he pulled it out of his pocket. But the call wasn't from his mother, letting him know where she was in traffic.

"Where are you?" the familiar voice demanded.

It was Rachel.

"Hello to you, too," he said. She was obviously extremely frustrated about something. Well, that made two of them.

"Sorry. Hi. Are you still on the ground?" she asked.

He glanced around. "Yeah. Your grandmother and my mom are running late."

"Where?" she asked, and he could hear the relief in her voice.

"On the tarmac, waiting for your grandmother and my mother to arrive and for the weather to clear.

"At the main terminal?" she pressed.

"No." He named the aviation company where he'd parked his plane and refueled. "Why?"

But she'd already disconnected. Colin stared at the dead phone in his hand, considered calling her cell, then simply closed the case. He didn't have the stomach for any more games. Just hearing her voice, albeit brief and sounding crazy, had been painful enough.

RACHEL RACED OUT of the main terminal at Newark Airport. Once she'd boarded the train at Penn Station, she'd made pretty good time to New Jersey.

Everyone knew that the trains moved faster than the auto traffic, which is why she hadn't hailed a cab. But she did now, directing the man to take her to the aviation company Colin had named. Ten minutes later the cabbie had dropped her off outside a large building and she headed toward the glass doors. She had no idea what was inside, but she wasn't afraid to ask questions and demand answers. She grasped the door handle the moment the wind picked up and the first raindrop fell.

"Rachel?"

She turned around, and saw her grandmother exit a big black Lincoln town car. Rachel went over to her. "Hi, Grandma. We need to get you inside. It's starting to rain."

"I can tell." Kim stepped aside to let Loretta Morris exit. Another fat raindrop fell and the women rushed inside just as the skies opened. "What are you doing here?" Kim asked. "You didn't have to come see us off."

"I'm hitching a ride home," Rachel declared. "I quit my job and I'm moving home. That is, if you'll still have me."

"This is rather sudden," Kim said. Loretta made her excuses and went to find the ladies' room.

Rachel knew her behavior appeared erratic. "Yes, it seems crazy, since I just got back here, but I know what I'm doing. Seriously. Please."

"Of course. I'd never turn you away, and Harold will be happy you're back to stay. He hasn't been the same since you stopped baking for me," Kim said. She appeared a bit smug, as if secretly pleased by something. "Are you sure this is what you want, though? What about New York?"

"I'm ready for something new," Rachel replied, relieved. "I guess a big city is just that when you don't have anyone to share it with. Oh, and remember that comment about Harold being happy, especially when you and I discuss the future of Kim's. I have a few ideas I'd like to try out."

"And I'm ready to entertain them," her grandmother said, cracking a wide smile. She hugged Rachel. "Welcome back."

Rachel trembled. One battle down. The next was the hard one, with no certain outcome.

By now Loretta had returned to the aviation company lobby, with its large lounge full of comfortable couches. A receptionist sat behind a huge counter.

"Oh, coffee. I want some of that," Loretta said, eyeing a restaurant-style coffeemaker with a fresh-brewed full pot.

"Help yourself. All beverages are complimentary," the receptionist said. She checked her screen. "Your plane is parked just out those doors and two down to the left. Very easy to reach, but with this weather, I have no idea when you'll take off," she said, addressing the older women.

"I want a cup of coffee, too," Kim said, and as both women moved to the refreshment stand, Rachel hurried to the exit opposite the doors through which they'd entered. The rain pelted her cheeks when she stepped outside, and the air wreaked havoc with her hair. She tried to tuck the locks behind her ears as she searched for Colin's plane.

The receptionist hadn't lied. He wasn't far, less than one hundred yards. She could see him sitting inside the Cessna, waiting for the rain to stop.

She quickened her pace and dodged raindrops as she ran around the front of the plane. She opened the passenger door and climbed in.

"Rachel?" Colin wore a shocked expression, and Rachel couldn't blame him. First, she was soaked. Second, he probably hadn't been expecting her.

"Hi," she said, wiping the wetness from her forehead. She rubbed the end of her nose and tried to calm frayed nerves. He appeared thinner, and there were circles under his eyes, as if he hadn't slept well. Still, to her, he appeared divine. "I ran into your mother and my grandmother inside. They're getting coffee."

"Well, we can't leave until the skies clear, anyway," he

said, immediately falling silent again as he attempted to figure out what this was all about. He wasn't giving her an inch, but who could blame him?

She took a deep breath. She had to try. It was now or never. "Got room for one more?"

Colin blinked furiously. "You're going to Morrisville? I guess I can take you. But how will you get back to New York?"

"I was hoping you'd help me with that, too," she rushed to say. "I thought maybe one of your friends could fly us both up sometime. It's a long, lonely drive and I'm really tired of being alone."

He held up his hands. "You're going to have to clarify. I might co-own a plane, but I'm not a taxi service at your disposal."

"No, but you *are* dense. I'm moving home. Permanently. As of this very minute. Or at least, when you can get this thing up in the air." The words burst forth in a jumble and she waited for his response.

He looked dumbfounded. "Why? This is New York. This is your dream. It's all you talked about."

"Was," she corrected him, realizing how much she loved him. She'd been such a fool. As Heather had said, anywhere was home when you were with the man you loved.

"My goal is to own my own bakery," Rachel told Colin. "I can't do that here. I've missed everyone. I've been so wrong. About everything. I've been deluding myself. I have a lot to tell you, the first of which is that I'm sorry about everything."

"So you think you can just apologize and that will change everything?"

She couldn't tell if he was joking or serious, so she addressed both possibilities. "I don't know if it will. But I'm willing to try. I'm willing to lay my heart on the line."

The airplane windows had fogged up. It was as if they were inside a bubble.

"I hurt you. I know that." She understood that she had an uphill battle. She'd left him for greener pastures after a week of lovemaking.

She had no magic wand to vanquish the pain of what she'd done. She would have to work hard to win him back, to prove she meant what she said. To prove that he was her other half and her future.

"We should probably check on Kim and my mom," he said.

"Can we talk later?" she asked.

"We'll see how later goes," he said, handing her an umbrella. He opened his door and got out.

Rachel sat there a moment and then followed him. But when they reached the lounge, neither Kim Palladia nor Loretta Morris was anywhere to be found.

Chapter Thirteen

First rain, then Rachel, now this. "The women in here earlier—where are they?" Colin asked the receptionist as Rachel came to stand beside him.

"Oh, they left with their limo driver, who was waiting around for a return fare into the city," the receptionist said.

At that moment, Colin's cell phone shrilled and he answered it. After listening for a moment, he hung up. He couldn't believe this. "That was my mom. She and Kim decided that since the storm would be around for a few more hours, they'd just go back to Manhattan and stay another night."

"Oh," Rachel said.

"Oh, yeah. It's not like I had to work tomorrow or anything."

"Sorry," Rachel said.

His shoulders slumped. As he exhaled, though, some of the tension left him. "Then again, my dad owns the place. I'm sure it will be fine. So why am I stressing?"

Because Rachel was standing next to him, wanting back into his life, that was why.

"A new weather brief just arrived," the receptionist said.

"The weather's supposed to be clear in about forty minutes. The front moved faster than expected."

"Let's go back to the plane," Colin said. They could talk there while he took a look at his charts.

The rain had almost stopped and Rachel climbed into the copilot's seat. The last time she'd sat next to him, they'd visited Chicago. Now here she was, flying home, to stay.

He wasn't sure if he could trust her declaration that she was returning permanently to Morrisville. The idea of Rachel settling down in a small town seemed so contradictory because she'd fled at the first opportunity. A thousand thoughts entered his head, all of them speculative. Maybe she'd been fired again. Had run into Marco. She'd said she couldn't open her own sweet shop in New York. Maybe that was the reason she was leaving a city she loved.

He glanced at her. "So you're back to stay," Colin said, breaking the silence.

"I am."

"Why?" he asked.

She sighed and Colin steeled himself. Here came the moment of truth. "There are lots of reasons. My grandmother dropped by to see me in New York. She was in and out like a whirlwind—which, I realized later, is how I used to visit my family and friends in Morrisville—I'd breeze in and breeze out."

She stopped for a moment, shaking her head. "Anyway, there I was on a Friday night, sitting in my hole-in-the-wall rented room. I don't really remember everything that she said, but her words made sense. I wasn't living the way I'd dreamed. I realized I've spent my whole life running away from Morrisville. It wasn't until two days ago that a huge fact struck me. Like blinders had been pulled off my eyes.

I never really appreciated everything I had there. I was so jaded from high school, so determined to escape, that I shut out all Morrisville's good qualities. I had to do that in order to delude myself that my life in New York was flawless and all I'd wanted."

"Nobody's life is perfect," Colin said.

"That's not what I meant. I have people in New York I can hang out with, but when I left, no one missed me. No one truly cared that I was gone, except maybe Marco, and that was because his pride was dented. It's not like he didn't move on quickly. I heard he's thinking about marrying his new girlfriend."

"I'm sorry," Colin said.

"Don't be. I'm not. Actually, I'm relieved. I was in love with a fairy tale. I told myself I was going to have my own bakery. I wanted to be like Sprinkles in L.A. or even as renowned as the Cheesecake Factory. But I was simply creating an illusion. I wasn't going to accomplish that. Not in New York. Not where I didn't have any true support."

She sighed before continuing. "I'm a third-generation cook. I have to live up to both my mother's and grandmother's reputations. I've been so afraid of being a failure, of not being good enough to be a part of Kim's, that I never tried to fit in in Morrisville. Not until February, when I had no other choice but to return. Did you know that Harold likes my bear claws better than my grandmother's? She told me that."

"My father thinks Harold's in love with your grandmother."

"That doesn't surprise me in the least. If he is, that makes his words even more meaningful. My baked goods *are* better than my grandmother's. That means I'm more than good enough. I'm not in anyone's shadow anymore."

"You never have been in the shadows," Colin protested.

"But in my mind I was. I thought you liked someone else. I worried that I'd never be good enough to take over the restaurant, and better I went somewhere else, someplace I had a clean slate. But this morning I realized that I could run a kitchen better than my horrid Bitsy's Bakery supervisor. The realization was like all the numbers on a slot machine lined up and there was the jackpot."

Colin didn't speak for a minute. "So you had a eureka moment? You couldn't have figured everything out before you broke my heart?" he asked finally.

"I hate myself for hurting you. I can't apologize enough, but I'll try."

"I'm not blaming you," he said softly. "I've been kicking myself. The best moments of my life were these past weeks with you, and they became like a one-night stand. You mean much more to me than that."

"I'm so sorry," she repeated.

"I did it to myself," he insisted.

At that moment, the rain stopped and the sun came out. "Perfect timing. We should be able to take off within the hour, depending on how backed up the runways are," he said.

"So can we begin again?" she asked. "You once told me that Marco's offer wasn't what we'd hoped for, but it wasn't the end of the world. Well, neither is this situation. I'm open for negotiation. I'm willing to come from my end if you're willing to give me another chance and come from yours. We'll end up where we want."

"And what is it that you want?" Colin asked, his gaze locking on to hers.

Rachel took a deep breath. "You."

COLIN SAT THERE a moment, savoring the one word she'd uttered. "I want you," she repeated, as if making certain he knew exactly how important this—he—was to her.

"What if you get bored? What if I'm not enough?" he pressed. He probably sounded like a cad, but he had to be certain.

"That's not going to happen. Home isn't a place. Home is being with the person you love, and that's you."

His heart skipped a beat. "You love me."

"Yes." She nodded and lowered her chin, almost as if embarrassed.

"You're not being very convincing." She glanced up then, looked at him. "I'm a lawyer. I'm a hard sell, especially given the evidence."

"What evidence? You don't believe your client's word?" she retorted.

Ah, there was the fighter he loved so much. His Rachel never quit. "I guess I'll have to reserve judgment," he said.

She leaned over, halfway into his space. "You can trust me. I'm here. I love you. I'm not leaving you ever again. That was the dumbest mistake of my life, and one I'm not repeating. You'd better get used to having me around, because I'm not going anywhere."

Exactly what he needed to hear. He covered her hand with his. "Thank you."

She used her free hand to sandwich his. "I love you. I just hope it isn't too late for you to fall in love with me again."

Men weren't supposed to cry, but Colin felt his eyes tear up. "I never stopped."

"No?"

He could hear the hope in her quivering voice. He shook

his head. "No. I've always loved you. I still do. You are the one I want to spend the rest of my life with."

"Can I kiss you now?" she asked.

Had any kiss been sweeter or more full of promise? His lips could taste the future. "As much as I hate to wait, we should take this somewhere more private. I believe you had some demands you wanted to make, and as your attorney, I'm ready to entertain them."

"My first is that you stop referring to yourself as my attorney," she said, kissing him again.

"So what am I to you?"

"Everything," she replied honestly. "And more. You are my man."

"I can live with that. Next demand?"

"That you take me home right now and make love to me. Your home, not mine," she clarified quickly. "I'm rather homeless. And I'd like to stay with you from this moment forward."

The skies were clearing and the rain had stopped, the fast-moving storm almost done passing through.

"Ah. I can grant that wish. We'll take off as soon as we get our family members back. We just need to *get* our family members back." He pressed her against him and gave her a long kiss.

"Good. Because I have a lot of plans to discuss with you."

"Sounds serious," he teased, enjoying the sensation of her body touching his.

"It is. You know how Morrisville likes to speculate."

"Oh, I do. I lose sleep over the gossip every night." Colin rolled his eyes.

She laughed at him. "You'll lose sleep, but not because of that. However, we'll have to discuss how to handle the grapevine. You see, Morrisville's going to have us hooked up and married off by next June. They'll give us a year, tops, before they'll be clamoring for us to walk down the aisle."

Colin made a mock-disgusted face. "Sounds horrible. I probably need to hide you quickly before anyone sees this embrace I'm sharing with you."

She winked at him. "You'll need to hide me only because what I'm about to do to you isn't fit for public viewing. As for the citizens of Morrisville, just beware. I'm siding with them. Your parents and mine might just get what they've always wanted."

She meant marriage, and Colin felt the last weight lift from his shoulders. He loved her. He didn't want one night or just a few months. He wanted forever. When the time was right, he'd surprise her with a ring. For now, the promise of a future was all the assurance he needed. "Well, I believe I told you that you belonged to me. That means I'm yours, as well. So next June, huh?"

"Uh-huh."

He grinned, happiness filling him. "I'm not afraid," he joked. "I've lived in Morrisville all my life. Shall we get going?" He reached for his phone to call his mother. He was ready to leave. Rachel was moving home. She'd marry him. She could start her Internet bakery, use Kim's Diner as a base of operations. And one day, just as Lancaster and Morris would be Colin's, Kim's Diner would be hers.

Hours later they drove up into Colin's driveway.

"Let's go inside," Colin said. "You have some promises to keep."

Rachel smiled and Colin knew they'd travel life's path together. At the moment, any appropriate quote slipped her mind, so she simply held his hand and gestured toward the door. "Yes. Let's."

And meeting in the middle, they took that first step.

Rachel's Recipe for Happiness

Start with multiple dashes of laughter, two hearts full of love, four handfuls of understanding.

Blend in heaps of patience, generosity and understanding, and then season with a bushel of tenderness.

Sprinkle generously with abundant kindness.

Add endless faith, hope and trust and mix well.

Set the timer to match a lifetime. You'll know you've achieved perfect results when you have multiple joyous memories that bring many smiles to your face.

Feel free to pass along this recipe to everyone you meet.

* * * * *

Look for LAST WOLF WATCHING
by Rhyannon Byrd—the exciting conclusion in
the BLOODRUNNERS miniseries
from Silhouette Nocturne.

Follow Michaela and Brody on their fierce journey
to find the truth and face the demons from the past,
as they reach the heart of the battle
between the Runners and the rogues.

Here is a sneak preview of book three,
LAST WOLF WATCHING.

Michaela squinted, struggling to see through the impenetrable darkness. Everyone looked toward the Elders, but she knew Brody Carter still watched her. Michaela could feel the power of his gaze. Its heat. Its strength. And something that felt strangely like anger, though he had no reason to have any emotion toward her. Strangers from different worlds, brought together beneath the heavy silver moon on a night made for hell itself. That was their only connection.

The second she finished that thought, she knew it was a lie. But she couldn't deal with it now. Not tonight. Not when her whole world balanced on the edge of destruction.

Willing her backbone to keep her upright, Michaela Doucet focused on the towering blaze of a roaring bonfire that rose from the far side of the clearing, its orange flames burning with maniacal zeal against the inky black curtain of the night. Many of the Lycans had already shifted into their preternatural shapes, their fur-covered bodies standing like monstrous shadows at the edges of the forest as they waited with restless expectancy for her brother.

Her nineteen-year-old brother, Max, had been attacked by a rogue werewolf—a Lycan who preyed upon humans for food. Max had been bitten in the attack, which meant he was no longer human, but a breed of creature that existed between the two worlds of man and beast, much like the Bloodrunners themselves.

The Elders parted, and two hulking shapes emerged from the trees. In their wolf forms, the Lycans stood over seven feet tall, their legs bent at an odd angle as they stalked forward. They each held a thick chain that had been wound around their inside wrists, the twin lengths leading back into the shadows. The Lycans had taken no more than a few steps when they jerked on the chains, and her brother appeared.

Bound like an animal.

Biting at her trembling lower lip, she glanced left, then right, surprised to see that others had joined her. Now the Bloodrunners and their family and friends stood as a united force against the Silvercrest pack, which had yet to accept the fact that something sinister was eating away at its foundation—something that would rip down the protective walls that separated their world from the humans'. It occurred to Michaela that loyalties were being announced tonight—a separation made between those who would stand with the Runners in their fight against the rogues and those who blindly supported the pack's refusal to face reality. But all she could focus on was her brother. Max looked so hurt…so terrified.

"Leave him alone," she screamed, her soft-soled, black satin slip-ons struggling for purchase in the damp earth as she rushed toward Max, only to find herself lifted off the ground when a hard, heavily muscled arm clamped around her waist from behind, pulling her clear off her feet. "Damn it, let me down!" she snarled, unable to take her eyes off her brother as the golden-eyed Lycan kicked him.

Mindless with heartache and rage, Michaela clawed at the arm holding her, kicking her heels against whatever part of her captor's legs she could reach. "Stop it," a deep, husky voice grunted in her ear. "You're not helping him by losing it. I give you my word he'll survive the ceremony, but you have to keep it together."

"Nooooo!" she screamed, too hysterical to listen to reason. "You're monsters! All of you! Look what you've done to him! How dare you! *How dare you!*"

The arm tightened with a powerful flex of muscle, cinching her waist. Her breath sucked in on a sharp, wailing gasp.

"Shut up before you get both yourself and your brother killed. I will *not* let that happen. Do you understand me?" her captor growled, shaking her so hard that her teeth clicked together. "Do you understand me, Doucet?"

"Damn it," she cried, stricken as she watched one of the guards grab Max by his hair. Around them Lycans huffed and growled as they watched the spectacle, while others outright howled for the show to begin.

"That's enough!" the voice seethed in her ear. "They'll tear you apart before you even reach him, and I'll be damned if I'm going to stand here and watch you die."

Suddenly, through the haze of fear and agony and outrage in her mind, she finally recognized who'd caught her. *Brody*.

He held her in his arms, her body locked against his powerful form, her back to the burning heat of his chest. A low, keening sound of anguish tore through her, and her head dropped forward as hoarse sobs of pain ripped from her throat. "Let me go. I have to help him. *Please*," she begged brokenly, knowing only that she needed to get to Max. "Let me go, Brody."

He muttered something against her hair, his breath warm against her scalp, and Michaela could have sworn it was a single word…. But she must have heard wrong. She was too upset. Too furious. Too terrified. She must be out of her mind.

Because it sounded as if he'd quietly snarled the word *never.*

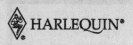

HARLEQUIN®

American ★ Romance®

Three Boys and a Baby

When Ella Garvey's eight-year-old twins and
their best friend, Dillon, discover an abandoned
baby girl, they fear she will be put in jail—
or worse! They decide to take matters into their
own hands and run away. Luckily the outlaws are
found quickly…and Ella finds a second chance
at love—with Dillon's dad, Jackson.

LOOK FOR

Three Boys and a Baby

BY

LAURA MARIE ALTOM

*Available May
wherever you buy books.*

LOVE, HOME & HAPPINESS

www.eHarlequin.com   HAR75215

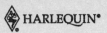
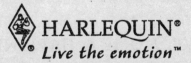

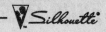

SPECIAL EDITION™

 THE WILDER FAMILY
Healing Hearts in Walnut River

Social worker Isobel Suarez was proud to
work at Walnut River General Hospital, so
when Neil Kane showed up from the attorney
general's office to investigate insurance fraud,
she was up in arms. Until she melted in his
arms, and things got very tricky...

Look for

HER MR. RIGHT?

by

KAREN ROSE SMITH

Available May wherever books are sold.

REQUEST YOUR FREE BOOKS!
2 FREE NOVELS PLUS 2
FREE GIFTS!

Heart, Home & Happiness!

YES! Please send me 2 FREE Harlequin American Romance® novels and my 2 FREE gifts (gifts are worth about \$10). After receiving them, if I don't wish to receive any more books, I can return the shipping statement marked "cancel." If I don't cancel, I will receive 4 brand-new novels every month and be billed just \$4.24 per book in the U.S. or \$4.99 per book in Canada, plus 25¢ shipping and handling per book and applicable taxes, if any*. That's a savings of close to 15% off the cover price! I understand that accepting the 2 free books and gifts places me under no obligation to buy anything. I can always return a shipment and cancel at any time. Even if I never buy another book from Harlequin, the two free books and gifts are mine to keep forever.

154 HDN EEZK 354 HDN EEZV

Name _____ (PLEASE PRINT)

Address _____ Apt. # _____

City _____ State/Prov. _____ Zip/Postal Code _____

Signature (if under 18, a parent or guardian must sign)

Mail to the **Harlequin Reader Service**:
IN U.S.A.: P.O. Box 1867, Buffalo, NY 14240-1867
IN CANADA: P.O. Box 609, Fort Erie, Ontario L2A 5X3

Not valid to current subscribers of Harlequin American Romance books.

Want to try two free books from another line?
Call 1-800-873-8635 or visit www.morefreebooks.com.

* Terms and prices subject to change without notice. N.Y. residents add applicable sales tax. Canadian residents will be charged applicable provincial taxes and GST. This offer is limited to one order per household. All orders subject to approval. Credit or debit balances in a customer's account(s) may be offset by any other outstanding balance owed by or to the customer. Please allow 4 to 6 weeks for delivery. Offer available while quantities last.

Your Privacy: Harlequin is committed to protecting your privacy. Our Privacy Policy is available online at www.eHarlequin.com or upon request from the Reader Service. From time to time we make our lists of customers available to reputable third parties who may have a product or service of interest to you. If you would prefer we not share your name and address, please check here. ☐

HAR08

HARLEQUIN *Presents*

Don't forget Harlequin Presents EXTRA
now brings you a powerful new collection
every month featuring four books!

Be sure not to miss any of the titles in

In the Greek Tycoon's Bed,

available May 13:

THE GREEK'S
FORBIDDEN BRIDE
by Cathy Williams

THE GREEK TYCOON'S
UNEXPECTED WIFE
by Annie West

THE GREEK TYCOON'S
VIRGIN MISTRESS
by Chantelle Shaw

THE GIANNAKIS BRIDE
by Catherine Spencer

® HARLEQUIN®

Mediterranean N I G H T S™

Sail aboard the glamorous Alexandra's Dream as the Mediterranean Nights series comes to its exciting conclusion!.

Coming in May 2008...

THE WAY HE MOVES

by
bestselling author

Marcia King-Gamble

As the sole heir to an affluent publishing company, Serena d'Andrea is very cautious when it comes to men. But a strange series of mishaps aboard *Alexandra's Dream* makes her wonder if someone is watching—and following—every move she makes. And when Gilles Anderson constantly seems to be coming to her rescue, she finds herself watching him.

Wherever books are sold starting the first week of May.

Look for the next exciting new 12-book series, Thoroughbred Legacy, in June 2008!

www.eHarlequin.com   HM38971

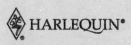

HARLEQUIN®

American ★ Romance®

COMING NEXT MONTH

#1209 THE FAMILY NEXT DOOR by Jacqueline Diamond
Harmony Circle
Josh Lorenz knows he's the last person Diane Bittner wants for a neighbor.
But their preteen daughters have a different opinion. And when the girls start
playing matchmaker for their clashing parents, Josh and Diane have to decide
what really matters. Reliving the mistakes of the past? Or planning their
future—together.

#1210 THE BEST MAN'S BRIDE by Lisa Childs
The Wedding Party
Colleen McCormick didn't expect to fall in love at her sister's wedding…and never
dreams sexy best man Nick Jameson feels the same way! Then the bride bails, and
Colleen and Nick are torn by divided loyalties. With the town of Cloverville up in
arms, the cynical Nick must decide if he trusts in love enough to make Colleen the
best man's bride.

#1211 THREE BOYS AND A BABY by Laura Marie Altom
When Ella Garvey's eight-year-old twins and their best friend Dillon discover
an abandoned baby girl, they fear she will be put in jail—or worse! They take
matters into their own hands and run away with the baby. Luckily the *outlaws*
are found quickly…and Ella finds a second chance at love—with Dillon's dad,
Jackson.

#1212 THE MOMMY BRIDE by Shelley Galloway
Motherhood
An unexpected pregnancy and a thirteen-year-old with an attitude complicate
matters when Claire Grant falls for Dr. Ty Slattery. Claire has had a rocky
past, making her wary of trusting anyone. But can the good doctor convince
her—and her son—that together they can be a family?

www.eHarlequin.com

HARCNM0408